The Weight of Escape

Unraveling Pain, Discovering Power

Amber L. Knightengale

Dedication

To my son, Brycen Shaw:

May you always know how deeply you are loved. Remember that you are covered by God's grace and, in times of loneliness or uncertainty, you can always turn to Him. You are a star, bright and unwavering, amazing in every way. No matter what challenges you may face, trust that everything will work out according to God's perfect plan for you. This story is a piece of my journey, but it's also a reminder of the strength, courage, and purpose that lie within you.

Acknowledgements

F irst and foremost, I want to thank God for his boundless blessings, encouragement, and guidance throughout my journey. His favor has been present over my life, my family, and this entire process, and I am forever grateful for his love, grace, and mercy. Writing this book has felt like a calling, a purpose I am meant to fulfill, and I am thankful for the green light he has given me to pursue this dream.

To my mom, whose gift for storytelling has inspired me to create worlds of my own. Your passion and dedication to writing have been a guiding light for me. Thank you for passing down this gift and showing me what it means to write with authenticity and heart.

To my son, Brycen Shaw—you are my joy, my strength, and my constant inspiration. This book, and every dream I pursue, is because of you. May you always know how amazing you are, covered by grace, destined for greatness, and loved beyond measure.

To my brothers, Stephon and Kris, thank you for your support and for always being there. To my nephews, Kaleb, Khalil, and Kyrie, and my nieces, Vanessa and Kamora —each of you brings so much joy and love into my life. I am incredibly proud to have you all as part of my journey.

To my auntie Sharon, who has been a precious part of my life since I was born. Growing up with you taught me patience, empathy, and an enduring capacity for love. Your presence has shaped me in ways I can't put into words.

To my auntie Gwen, who is no longer with us but whose strength, beauty, and power continue to guide me. You taught me resilience and perseverance, always holding a special place for me in your heart. Though you are not here, you will forever hold a special place in mine.

To my grandmother, Jessie Mae Plunkett, whom I, unfortunately, never had the chance to meet, but whose legacy of strength and beauty has deeply influenced me. From what I've learned, you were the matriarch of our family, an incredible woman who raised eleven children with resilience and grace, enduring and overcoming challenges with unwavering love. Though we never met, I feel close to you, and I know you watch over me. Your spirit continues to inspire me, and I am forever grateful for the legacy of courage and compassion you've left behind.

To my family and friends who have supported me along this journey, thank you for being my foundation. Your love and encouragement have given me the strength to see this dream through. This book is a testament to all of you, and I am endlessly grateful.

And finally, to each person who has been part of my story—through friendship, challenge, or love—thank you. Every chapter of my life is richer because of you.

Disclaimer

This book is a work of fiction. While inspired by a blend of personal life experiences and imagination, the characters, incidents, dialogues, and settings have been modified, fictionalized, or created solely for the purpose of storytelling. Any resemblance to actual persons, living or dead, or to actual events, is purely coincidental.

The narrative explores universal themes of personal growth, relationships, and self-discovery, and incorporates dramatized events and interactions. While some elements may reflect real-life experiences of the author, all characters are composites, and certain events have been altered, enhanced, or fully fictionalized to serve the book's themes and narrative arc.

This story is intended to resonate emotionally with readers and is not intended as an account of any particular person or event. Readers are reminded to view all people, places, and events within this story as fictional constructs, brought to life through the author's creative lens.

Introduction

"The Weight of Escape" is a story shaped by emotional truths, some lived, some imagined, and the quiet, often unseen journeys we take within ourselves. The characters and experiences in these pages are drawn from moments felt, observed, and remembered, shaped by the imprints of heartbreak, memory, and growth. They are not just names on a page, but emotional landscapes—fragments of pain, longing, love, loss, hope, and resilience.

This story captures more than a journey of escape; it's a journey of healing and self-discovery. In life, we all face moments when the weight feels unbearable, when our first instinct is to run—to escape. But as Seven learns, and as I've come to understand, true freedom isn't found in running away. It's in facing those moments head-on, allowing ourselves to feel the depth of the pain, learning from it, and ultimately letting it shape us into someone stronger and more resilient.

We all experience moments of unhappiness, regret, and heartache. Those feelings are part of being human. But growth comes when we refuse to let those moments define us and, instead, find ways to move forward, carrying with us the lessons they taught. Life doesn't ask for perfection, nor does healing mean we won't still feel sadness or have regrets. It's about accepting those emotions, letting them guide us toward a deeper understanding of ourselves, and finding peace in the present.

"The Weight of Escape" invites you to walk with Seven, and with me, through the highs and lows, the heartbreak and hope, as we each strive to make sense of our journeys. This story is a reminder that while escape may be our first instinct, facing our realities, learning, and growing from them is the true path to freedom. It's okay to want to escape. But it's also okay to stay, to heal, and to live fully, embracing all the beauty and struggle life offers while we're here.

Author's Bio

A mber L. Knightengale is a devoted mother, successful career woman, and now a published author, passionate about creating stories that resonate with readers on a deep, emotional level. With a goal to achieve even greater success, she balances her professional accomplishments with a fulfilling personal life, cherishing the moments spent with her child. With an adventurous spirit and a deep sense of curiosity, Amber embraces challenges and views each one as an opportunity for growth.

Deeply rooted in her spirituality, Amber navigates life through the guidance of God, prayer, and meditation, which serve as the foundation of her strength and creativity. Her debut novel, The Weight of Escape, reflects her belief in the power of resilience and self-discovery. The book was inspired by some personal experiences and her desire to connect with readers facing their own battles.

Amber is also passionate about giving back through meaningful service and supporting underserved communities with compassion and care. From community outreach and meal support, to mentoring and motivating loved ones, she embodies the belief that we all thrive when we uplift one another. Through her writing, she hopes to inspire readers to find their own strength and embrace the possibilities that life offers.

Table of Contents

1. The Weight of Betrayal   1

2. Unraveling the Past   7

3. The Weight of Love   15

4. Echo's of the Past   28

5. Distant Memories   37

6. Family Ties   50

7. A Fragile Foundation   58

8. Shadows Beneath the Surface   68

9. Whispers Along the Path   78

10. Confronting the Abyss   86

11. The Weight of Wishes   92

12. A New Path   98

13. Embracing the Journey   104

14. The Edge of Everything   110

15. Strange Encounter   117

16. Are you Awake   125

17. Journey Back   132

18. A Change in Perspective   138

19. The Still Point   144

20. After the Weight   150

21. In the Wake of Escape   155

1

The Weight of Betrayal

The quiet was oppressive, unsettling. Seven sat alone in the dim light of her kitchen, the walls closing in around her like the weight of the bills scattered across the table. A mountain of papers loomed before her, unfinished projects, work obligations, her mounting responsibilities. The glaring light overhead flickered, casting shadows that danced ominously along the walls. But one document that stood out among the rest, its starkness cutting through the haze of her thoughts. It was a child support check slip from Rowan, her child's father.

As Seven traced the familiar handwriting, remembering his past promises, her heart grew heavy. Promises of love, of support, of a future together. Promises that became dust, leaving her feeling betrayed and alone. She thought of their daughter, Ryan, who deserved so much more than the chaotic mess Rowan had left behind.

The months turned into years, and Rowan's presence in their lives had been a roller-coaster of emotions. His lies, so seamlessly woven into their interactions, became part of the fabric of their relationship. He had insisted, over and over, that he was not married, that he was single, that they had a future together. She had believed him. After all, when you love someone, you want to see the best in them. But as her pregnancy progressed, reality crept in, casting shadows on their dreams.

When Seven first discovered she was pregnant, Rowan was there, seemingly supportive, attending doctor appointments, texting her during the late nights when she couldn't sleep. He was the perfect partner; she thought. The man who promised he would be there for her and their baby. She began to picture a future where they were a family, a perfect little unit. But those moments of warmth were fleeting.

As the months of her pregnancy wore on, something shifted. Rowan's attention shifted, just slightly at first, so small that she almost didn't notice. But soon, those small changes became impossible to ignore. His calls became less frequent, his texts more distant. He still sent the occasional "I love you" messages, but they felt hollow, as if he'd written them in a rush. Her growing belly seemed to separate them further, like an invisible wall she couldn't breach. She made excuses for him, telling herself he was just busy with work, or stressed about his own life. After all, they had so much to look forward to. The baby. Their future. But every passing day, a subtle disconnect grew between them.

She could feel him slipping away, though she didn't know why. She kept herself busy, preparing for the baby, organizing the nursery, but the loneliness seeped in. The quiet whispers of doubt crept into her mind, telling her something was wrong. She pushed them aside. Rowan had always been a man of his word, or at least that's what she believed.

One evening, when Seven was six months along, she did what she never thought she'd have to do: she searched his name online. She was standing in the kitchen, absentmindedly scrolling through social media, when a name caught her eye—Rowan Thomas. His name appeared in a family photo. Smiling, surrounded by children who looked just like him, with a woman by his side who seemed to glow with familiarity. His wife. The woman who had existed in the shadows of their relationship all along.

Her breath caught in her throat as the image burned into her memory. The bright smiles, the way he held his wife's hand. She stared at the screen, her heart pounding in her chest. How had she never seen this? How had he lied to her for months, no, years about his marriage? He'd insisted he was single, that he was going through a rough patch, that things weren't what they seemed. But here it was, in black and white; his life, his wife, and his children, all of it hidden from her.

Anger surged through her, but an aching, hollow emptiness quickly replaced it. She had been living a lie. And worse, she had been foolish enough to believe him.

Seven clicked on the profile, scrolling through picture after picture. There they were, Rowan with his wife and kids, their life unfolding in the posts like a painful reminder of everything she had hoped for but would never have. The future she had imagined for herself and Ryan felt like a distant dream, shattered by the cruel truth.

She sat down at the kitchen table. The overhead light mocked her with its flickering, casting dancing shadows. It was as though the room had gotten smaller, the air thicker with the weight of her realization. Rowan had lied about everything. He wasn't just deceitful; he was masterful. She had been a fool to trust him.

And yet, despite everything, she couldn't bring herself to feel the anger she thought would consume her. No, it was a quiet devastation that took hold of her. She questioned everything the past year, the months of her pregnancy, and the future she had been planning. Everything had been built on a foundation of lies.

The worst part was her inability to tell anyone. How could she? How could she explain to her family, her friends, that the man who had promised to help raise her child was a stranger? How could she admit such naivete, believing his professed love was genuine?

She already envisioned the pity in her mother's eyes. She heard the "I told you so" from her brother. No one had believed in Rowan. No one had ever trusted him the way she had. They were right, and now she bears the consequences of that misplaced faith.

Seven stayed up late that night, scrolling through Rowan's online presence until her eyes burned from exhaustion. Each post felt like a cruel slap. She had been nothing more than a side story in his life, a passing affair. But she was so wrapped up in his words and the need for his love, for companionship, that she had blinded herself to the truth.

Following the revelation of Rowan's secret, Seven's pregnancy became a blur, lasting several weeks. She went through the motions, doctor appointments, the baby shower, the final preparations for Ryan's arrival; yet all the while, broken inside. Rowan didn't call, didn't check in. He didn't even acknowledge the fact that she had found out about his family. Seven was forced to finish out her pregnancy in isolation, knowing that the man she had trusted had abandoned her. She could barely bring herself to leave the house, feeling like everyone around her was watching, waiting for her to collapse.

Every day, she felt the weight of her grief dragging her down, but she kept going. She couldn't stop. She had a child to think of now, a baby girl who deserved better. Ryan needed her to stay strong, even if it felt like every part of her was crumbling. So, she swallowed her heartbreak and pushed forward.

When Ryan finally arrived, Seven held her baby in her arms with a quiet strength, knowing that her world had shifted in ways she couldn't yet understand. Ryan deserved a father who would show up, who would protect her and love her. But that was something Rowan could never give her.

Rowan's absence wasn't just physical, it was a betrayal of the deepest kind. Seven served as a placeholder in his life, a temporary distraction from whatever chaos he was dealing with. But to her, Ryan was everything. She would do whatever it took to protect her from the darkness that had surrounded her, from the lies and deceit Rowan had woven into her life.

The months went by, and life with Ryan was both beautiful and terrifying. Seven took on the responsibility of being a mother alone, but somehow, that only solidified her determination to give her daughter the life she deserved. Still, in the quiet moments when she looked at her baby, she couldn't help but wonder how Rowan could have disappeared so completely. The man she thought she knew was now a stranger, a shadow in her past that she couldn't escape.

Her fingers brushed over the ink of the child support check, tracing the letters like a bitter reflex. Her mind drifted, unbidden, to a time when his words had carried promise instead of betrayal. A time when she'd believed in him.

"You're different, Sev," Rowan said one evening as they sat by the lake near her apartment. He had a way of looking at her that made her feel like the only person in the world. "You don't ask for much. I like that about you."

Seven had blushed at the time, too flattered to notice the weight of his words. Now, years later, they echoed in her mind with an entirely different meaning. You don't ask for much. Of course, he had liked that. It had made it easier for him to take giving nothing in return.

Back then, Rowan had been everything she thought she prayed for. Charming, attentive, quick to share his dreams about the future. He had a way of weaving his words into something so tangible she could almost touch it. And she wanted to touch it. To believe in it.

"You ever think about having kids?" he'd asked once, tracing circles on her wrist as they lay tangled together on her couch.

"All the time," she'd replied without hesitation. "I want a big family someday. Lots of love, lots of noise."

"Yeah," he'd said, his voice distant. "Me too. Someday."

But Seven knew something now. Something she had to hold on to. Her life was hers to shape. She would not let Rowan's betrayal define her any longer. She would escape the suffocating grip of her past and make a future for herself and Ryan, even if it meant walking away from everything that had been.

One night, as she lay in bed, staring at the ceiling, she made a vow to herself. She would reclaim her life. No matter the cost. No matter the challenge. Seven would build a new future.

Little did she know, the journey ahead would be nothing like she expected. The world outside, the one she thought she was escaping, would throw itself at her in ways she couldn't yet imagine.

And she would soon learn there was more to her strength than she ever realized.

2

Unraveling the Past

Seven sat at the edge of her bed, her thoughts tangled in the complexity of everything that had happened. She glanced at Ryan, napping in the next room, blissfully unaware of the emotional whirlwind that had been wreaking havoc on her mother's heart. As Seven let her gaze wander, she couldn't help but think back on Rowan. This was the man who had once occupied her thoughts, her heart, and her life.

Rowan's goodness as a father to his two other children was undeniable. He worked hard, showed up, and provided for them in ways that many people could only wish for. He was reliable with his other children. This steadiness contrasted with his darker qualities. Rowan's capacity for love almost intertwined with his ability to deceive. In the moments when he was with his kids, when he was being the dad he had never been for Seven, she saw a side of him she wanted to believe in, maybe a side of him he buried so deep inside himself. He was dependable in that way. He had this capability of being a provider and protector, even if the other parts of him were so far removed from the man Seven had once thought him to be.

But then there was the other side of Rowan, the side she had seen clearly: manipulative, deceitful, cold. His charm could mask his dark tendencies, but with each layer she uncovered, Seven realized that the man she had loved, and still couldn't seem to fully let go of, had been someone else entirely. Rowan was a walking contradiction, someone who wore confidence like armor, yet underneath, he was fragile, insecure. His coldness, his ability to lie without remorse, had been his defense against a world he couldn't trust.

And perhaps, she realized with growing discomfort, part of her was drawn to that side of him, the darkness that lived in him mirrored the part of herself she had never acknowledged; the part of her that had always felt bruised by life but never quite understood why. Why does his darkness feel so familiar? She wondered.

A Dark Resonance

Seven had never been the emotional type. As a child, emotions had felt more like luxuries than necessities. Her mother, overburdened with work and worry, hadn't had the time to comfort a tearful daughter. Seven learned early that tears didn't solve problems, that sadness didn't pay bills, and that anger only made you a target. Shutting down was safer, more efficient. It allowed her to move through life without the weight of vulnerability pulling her under.

But that strength had come at a price. Emotional self-sufficiency left her isolated, even when surrounded by others. Her stoicism became both her shield and her prison. It was no wonder, then, that Rowan's boldness, his refusal to be tethered by guilt or consequence, had struck a chord deep within her.

Was I drawn to Rowan's dark side? She wondered now, sitting in the dim light of her kitchen. His audacity had been magnetic, a quality that made the world bend to his will. It wasn't just confidence—confidence could be learned, rehearsed. Rowan possessed something more primal: an unshakable belief that he could take what he wanted and the world would somehow accommodate him.

It struck a chord in Seven, a part of herself she rarely admitted, the part that longed for that kind of freedom. She had spent her life suppressing her own desires, molding herself to meet others' expectations. Seeing Rowan break the rules she had so dutifully followed was both maddening and deeply alluring.

Yet Seven had always known there was more to Rowan than his bravado. Rowan was broken beneath the surface. She had seen glimpses of it in the quiet moments, when his laughter gave way to silence or when his confident facade cracked just enough to reveal the man underneath. Rowan wore his pain like armor, a heavy shield forged from past betrayals and self-inflicted wounds.

And part of her admired that. Maybe even envied it. His ability to channel his hurt into a shield of indifference was something she couldn't master. Seven carried her wounds inward, where they festered in silence, but Rowan's pain was visible, tangible. It gave him a dangerous allure, like watching a fire and knowing you should step back but being unable to look away.

She remembered the first time she'd seen that vulnerability. They had been sitting in her apartment, the quiet evening that made the world outside feel far away. Rowan was leaning against the counter, a glass of whiskey in his hand, his usual charm dampened by some invisible weight.

"You ever feel like life's just a game you're destined to lose?" he'd asked, his voice uncharacteristically soft.

The question had caught her off guard. "What do you mean?"

He had shrugged, his gaze distant. "Like no matter what you do, no matter how hard you try, it's never enough. You're always playing catch-up."

Seven had studied him, searching for the Rowan she knew, the one who always seemed so sure of himself, so untouchable. But in that moment, he looked... human.

"I think everyone feels like that sometimes," she'd said cautiously.

"Not like this." He'd laughed bitterly, taking a long sip of his drink. "It's like... I don't know how to stop running. Like if I stop, everything will fall apart."

She had wanted to comfort him, to tell him he didn't have to run anymore, but the words had felt hollow even in her mind. Instead, she'd reached for his hand, offering the only solace she could.

That night had stayed with her, not because of what he'd said, but because of what it revealed about her own heart. Seven had always prided herself on being the strong one, the one who didn't ask for help or lean on others. But Rowan's brokenness mirrored something she had long buried within herself, the fear that her own strength was just a facade, a brittle mask hiding fractures she was too afraid to examine.

Was that what I had been looking for all along? She wondered now. Someone who was both strong and broken? Someone I could fix?

She hated the implication; that her love for Rowan had been less about him and more about her own unresolved wounds made her stomach churn. But the truth was undeniable. Rowan had been a mirror, reflecting the parts of herself she had tried so hard to ignore.

There had been moments when their connection felt like destiny, as though their shared scars bound them together. Rowan's darkness had a gravitational pull, drawing her in despite the warning signs. She could see the cracks in his armor, the way he deflected rather than confronted his pain, and she had convinced herself that she could help him heal.

"You can't fix people, Sev," her best friend, Lila, had told her once. "You're not a bandage, and you're not a therapist."

"I'm not trying to fix him," Seven had protested, though even as she said it, the words felt like a lie.

"Then what are you doing?" Lila had asked, her tone both concerned and exasperated.

Seven hadn't had an answer. Not then.

Rowan's contradictions were as addictive as they were, infuriating. His strength gave her something to lean on, while his vulnerability made her feel needed. It was a dangerous mix, blurring the line between love and self-destruction.

She could still hear his voice in her mind, the way he would say her name like it held some secret power. "You're different, Sev," he had told her more than once. "You're so easy-going and you don't ask for much."

She had taken it as a compliment. She had thought it meant he valued her simplicity, her ability to find contentment without demanding more. But now, years later, the words echoed with a bitterness she couldn't ignore.

Seven leaned back in her chair, the weight of her reflections pressing against her chest. She had spent so long trying to untangle Rowan's complexities, trying to understand what had drawn her to him and why she couldn't seem to let go. But perhaps the real question wasn't about Rowan at all.

Why does his darkness feel so familiar?

The answer lingered just out of reach, like a shadow she couldn't quite catch. But one thing was clear: Rowan wasn't just a man she had loved and lost. He reflected the parts of herself she still didn't understand, the wounds she hadn't healed, the strength she had forged from pain, and the longing for connection that had led her into his arms.

To understand him, Seven realized, she would first have to understand herself, and that was the most complicated puzzle of all.

The Mystery of Rowan and the Mystery of Herself

Rowan was a mystery. People often saw him as the life of the party, charming, confident, even cocky. But when you looked past the facade, it was easy to see that he wasn't as unshakable as he appeared. There were moments when he seemed to unravel, when the weight of his own lies would catch up with him. And when that happened, Seven would catch glimpses of the man behind the mask; the real man, the one who had never committed to the idea of love or family, the one who had chosen survival over the connection.

And yet, Seven couldn't bring herself to hate him. Why? she asked herself. Why did she still feel this pull, this lingering attachment to someone who had caused her so much pain?

Mystery had always drawn her in, and Rowan, for all his flaws, was the embodiment of it. He lingered just beyond her grasp, always keeping part of himself hidden, even after everything they'd been through. His complexity both infuriated and intrigued her, and a part of her couldn't help but want to unravel him.

It wasn't just Rowan who had been a mystery, though. I've been a mystery too, haven't I? Seven thought, reflecting on her own emotional withdrawal. In her earlier dating life, she had been the one people couldn't quite figure out, the one who kept her cards close to her chest, never revealing too much. She had been too strong, too self-sufficient, too guarded.

That had always been a defense mechanism, a way of protecting herself from the disappointment and heartbreak she had so often experienced. But now, looking back, Seven could see the way her walls had kept her from experiencing love in its purest form. She had always expected too little from others, afraid to trust because of the pain she had endured. Rowan's darkness had mirrored her own, and that strange connection between them, that magnetism, was what kept pulling her back in.

Rowan, the Father

Rowan wasn't just a part of Seven's life because of their turbulent past; he was part of her present because of Ryan. Seven knew that no matter how much pain Rowan had caused her, she could never erase him from her life. He was Ryan's father, and for that reason alone, Seven would have to coexist with him.

Ryan meant the world to her. Although she resented Rowan's lies, she couldn't deny he'd given her the greatest gift: her daughter. It didn't make sense, but it was true. Without him, there would be no Ryan.

Seven wrestled with that paradox daily. Rowan had betrayed her trust, manipulated her, and led her down a path she didn't choose. But he had also given her Ryan, and in some strange way, she owed him for that. Ryan was the one thing that had brought meaning to all the chaos, the one light that had come from the darkness.

Protecting the Monster

Seven's internal battle was exhausting. She couldn't completely walk away from Rowan, and she couldn't forgive him, either. He had ruined parts of her life, but he had also given her Ryan. And despite everything, Seven couldn't bring herself to destroy him. There were secrets, things he had told her, things he had done that could easily tear apart his world. But she had never told a soul. She never would.

It wasn't about protecting him; it was about something deeper, something she couldn't quite put into words. What does it say about me, that I want to protect someone who has caused me so much pain?

Seven couldn't answer that. All she knew was that the strange alliance she had formed with Rowan, the bond they shared because of Ryan, had shaped her in ways she hadn't realized. Their connection defied logic and reason. It wasn't just about the lies or the betrayal, it was about the deeper, spiritual connection that came with creating life together, even if that life had come from such a messy and painful place.

A Monster, A Love

In the end, Seven had to come to terms with something that felt impossible: she loved a monster.

And that realization made her question everything. What does that make me? A part of her wanted to run from the answer, wanted to shove it aside and pretend it wasn't true. But she couldn't. The truth was evident now. She had been drawn to Rowan's darkness, and in some ways, her own darkness had been drawn to him. They had fed each other's pain, each other's wounds. But Ryan was the light that had come out of it all, and in that, Seven had to find some measure of peace.

As she sat on the porch one evening, looking out at the world that felt so far removed from the chaos she had once known. Seven ultimately accepted that she would never fully untangle herself from Rowan. She didn't need to. What mattered was that she had Ryan now, and that was enough to start anew. The journey wasn't over, and it never would be. But for the first time in years, Seven felt like she was ready to move forward.

3

The Weight of Love

A t an emotional crossroads, Seven grappled with the indelible marks two men had left on her soul. Michael and Rowan, their names echoed in her thoughts like haunting refrains in a bittersweet melody. Each had shaped her life in ways she couldn't ignore, their presence a mixture of beauty and destruction that had left her emotionally unmoored. In Seven's eyes, Michael was her soulmate, while Rowan, her child's father, held a divinely ordained connection due to their shared child.

She thought about the love she had once believed was pure and enduring, and how it had crumbled into something unrecognizable. With Michael, there had been moments so sweet they felt timeless, as if the two of them existed in a bubble that nothing could penetrate. But that love had come with an edge, sharp, cutting, and always reminding her that nothing truly lasts. Rowan, on the other hand, had been a spark of something new, a promise of escape, only to reveal himself as another man with secrets and a knack for breaking hearts.

The dim light of the kitchen flickered overhead, casting long shadows that seemed to mirror the doubts in her mind. She stared at the empty chair across the table, the hollow space seeming to mock her. How many nights had she imagined Michael sitting there, his familiar smirk fading into a warm smile? How many mornings had she envisioned Rowan sharing breakfast with her and Ryan, pretending the world wasn't as complicated as it truly was?

Her chest tightened as her thoughts spiraled. She had spent years investing in men who couldn't, or wouldn't, give her the same in return. The void at the table wasn't just physical; it was emotional, spiritual. It was a reflection of the emptiness she had been trying to fill for so long, a space carved out by love that never stayed.

Ryan's laughter from the next room broke through the fog in her mind, a melody so pure it pulled her back to the present. The sound was like sunlight streaming through a cracked window, offering a glimpse of warmth in a cold, shadowed room. Seven closed her eyes for a moment, letting the joy of her daughter's voice wash over her.

Her daughter was her anchor, her reason. Yet, even Ryan's light couldn't fully chase away the questions that lingered.

How had she allowed herself to endure so much?

She thought of Michael, of the nights she lay awake waiting for a text, a call, some sign that he cared as much as she did. She remembered the way he could charm her, his smile disarming, his words smooth as silk, even when they were lying. Michael had a way of making her feel special, but only in moments that were convenient for him. When he wasn't around, and his attention was elsewhere, she felt like a forgotten page in a book he had stopped reading.

Why had she held on to Michael's empty promises for so long?

She hated how deeply she had loved him, how she had clung to the idea that he was her person, the one meant for her. She hated the way his fleeting presence still had the power to ignite something in her, even after all the heartbreak.

And then there was Rowan.

Why had she let Rowan's betrayal burrow so deeply into her heart?

His lies had blindsided her, shattering the fragile trust she had so willingly given him. He made her feel wanted, cherished even, only to reveal himself as a man with a double life and a family he had conveniently forgotten to mention. And yet, she couldn't completely hate him. He had given her Ryan, her greatest blessing, and for that, she felt an inexplicable gratitude that warred with her resentment.

Seven let out a shaky breath, her shoulders slumping as she rested her head in her hands. The answers weren't coming, not tonight. They never came when she searched for them. They lingered just out of reach, teasing her with the promise of clarity she might never have.

She raised her head and glanced at the table again, her thoughts unraveling further. The emptiness was more than physical; it was symbolic. She had poured so much of herself into these men, into relationships that had left her drained, and now she was left to piece herself back together.

A Love That Was Never Enough

Michael had been apart of Seven's life since they were teenagers, and from the moment they met, he had swept her off her feet with a kind of magnetic charm that left her breathless. He had a boyish smile that disarmed her, a laugh that seemed to promise the world, and a way of looking at her like she was the only person in the room. When she was seventeen, Seven believed in fairytales, and to her, Michael was the prince who made her believe that their love story would last forever.

But fairytales weren't real.

Over time, Michael's love became a riddle Seven couldn't solve. He would draw her close with his warmth, only to pull away when she reached for him. His words were sweet and intoxicating, but his actions never followed through. She learned to brace herself for the emotional whiplash he brought, his cold and hot energy keeping her off balance.

For all his charm, Michael was a man of contradictions. He could make her feel like she was the center of his universe one day and a passing thought the next. Their chemistry was undeniable, intense, electric, and impossible to ignore. He could make her laugh until her stomach hurt, his quick wit matching hers effortlessly. Yet, for every moment of connection, there were countless instances of doubt and abandonment.

Seven often replayed those moments in her mind, searching for clues as to why his love seemed to run so hot and cold. She remembered the nights they spent talking for hours, the way his voice softened when he told her about his dreams, and how he once kissed her on the forehead and whispered, "You're my favorite person in the world."

But then there were the other nights. The ones where she waited for his call that never came, her stomach in knots as she checked her phone every few minutes. The ones where he disappeared without explanation, only to return weeks later with a nonchalant smile, as if nothing had happened.

"Why can't you just commit?" Seven's voice echoed in her memory, the question a plea she had asked a hundred times before. She hated how her voice had cracked, revealing the vulnerability she tried so hard to hide.

Michael always responded the same way, his tone full of feigned sincerity. "It's not you, Seven. You're perfect. It's me. I'm just not in the right place for something serious."

It wasn't the words themselves that hurt, it was the way he said them, as though they were meant to console her when they only twisted the knife deeper. Seven knew better than to believe him, but a part of her wanted to. His excuses were maddeningly consistent, and she hated how they made her feel like the problem wasn't him but her.

Michael's love had always been conditional, a prize he doled out sparingly, leaving Seven feeling like she had to earn it. And she tried, God, how she tried. She became the woman she thought he wanted: attentive, patient, and understanding. But no matter how much of herself she gave, it was never enough.

Seven thought about how unworthy Michael had made her feel. His mixed signals left her questioning her own worth, wondering what she lacked that kept him from choosing her. She couldn't shake the feeling that she was always auditioning for a role she would never get, the one where she was finally his partner, his equal.

There was a particular night that lingered in her memory, a moment that epitomized their relationship. They had been at a party, surrounded by friends and family, the air thick with laughter and music. Michael had spent most of the evening by her side, his arm casually draped around her shoulders, his presence making her feel like they were a team.

But as the night wore on, Michael drifted away from her, pulling out his phone and typing furiously. Seven noticed the change in his behavior, his body language was open and relaxed, his focus entirely on the screen. She caught a glimpse of the words, a name, the playful tone of the messages. He was texting another woman, and it struck her like a slap across the face. The ease with which he was engaging, the way he seemed so absorbed in the conversation—it made her stomach churn.

She tried to brush it off, convincing herself that she was overreacting, that it was just a message. But deep down, she knew better. The way his smile softened at the screen, the way he responded with that familiar warmth, it wasn't just casual conversation. It felt intimate, like something more. It was the same way he had texted her when they first started, the way he made her feel special, only now it wasn't for her.

The knot in her stomach grew tighter, and she could feel the anger rising, but she kept it in check. She didn't want to make a scene, didn't want to be the paranoid girlfriend. But the image of him texting someone else kept nagging at her, gnawing at her insides.

After a few minutes, she couldn't stand it any longer. She walked over to where he sat, his eyes glued to his phone, and when he looked up, she asked softly, "Who are you texting?"

His eyes darkened for a moment. Guilt maybe, but he smothered it quickly with a practiced grin. "Just a friend," he said casually, tapping the phone with his thumb. "Nothing serious."

Seven's heart sank, but she wasn't about to back down. "A friend? Really?" Her voice barely rose above a whisper, but it carried the weight of everything she was feeling, the frustration, the hurt, the years of questioning his intentions.

Michael chuckled, leaning back in his chair. "You're overreacting, Seven," he said, his voice smooth and effortless. "You know you're the one I care about. It's just a message."

The dismissiveness in his tone hit harder than the words themselves. Seven stood there, feeling the sting of betrayal, her heart pounding in her chest. She had been here before, where his words didn't align with his actions, where his love felt conditional and unreliable.

She wanted to scream, to demand the truth, to tell him how much this hurt. But instead, she felt the familiar weight of resignation settle over her. He'll never change, she thought. He'll never choose me fully.

Seven swallowed the bitter pain and nodded, her throat tight. "Yeah, okay," she murmured, turning to walk away, but she ever never forgot that moment.

The Breaking Point

There was another night that stood out in Seven's memory, a night that still sent shivers down her spine whenever it crossed her mind. This night led to the breaking point. It had started out like any other argument, with Michael's words cutting through the air like they had so many times before. But this time, it felt different. The tension was sharper, the air heavier.

They had been fighting for what felt like hours, both of them too exhausted from the cycle of miscommunication, both too proud to back down. Michael accused her of being too demanding, too intense, as if her need for commitment, for security, was somehow unreasonable. And that was when it happened, the words that she had been holding inside, the frustration of years of emotional neglect, spilled out in a rush of anger. He even had the audacity to say she couldn't be trusted because of her ways earlier in their relationship, but Seven counted it as just another excuse.

"You're a coward," she had spat, the words laced with years of resentment. "You use your insecurities as an excuse to hurt people, and I'm done letting you hurt me."

The moment the words left her mouth, she saw it, the smirk on his face. The same smirk that always made her feel small, like her pain, was a joke to him. That smirk was the final straw, the one thing that pushed her over the edge. Seven didn't even think; her body acted on its own. She turned, grabbed a knife from the counter, and without a second thought, she bolted out the door after him.

The cool night air stung against her skin, but it was nothing compared to the fire in her chest, the heat of fury that was now consuming her. Barefoot, she sprinted down the street, her heart pounding, her thoughts scattered. But one thing was clear—she needed him to understand.

Michael had already reached the end of the driveway when he turned around, his voice filled with panic and disbelief. "Seven, what the hell are you doing?"

She didn't answer. She couldn't. The words simply weren't there. There was nothing left to explain, nothing left to justify. All that remained was the desperate hope that he might finally see her pain and feel the full weight of what he had put her through.

"Seven!" His voice shook her from the fog of rage, and she stopped, standing there in the middle of the street, the knife trembling in her hand. The reality of what she had just done hit her like a freight train. She was standing there, holding a knife, in the middle of the street, barefoot and shaking, but for what?

The cool air cut through the fury, and with it, a sense of shame washed over her. What had she become? The person standing before Michael was not the woman she recognized, the woman who had always prided herself on her strength and composure. She had let him break her in a way she never thought possible.

The night dragged on, but the argument had lost its meaning. The words Michael had said, the accusations and the blame, were forgotten in the haze of her own shame. What lingered was the feeling of being undone, exposed in a way she hadn't known existed. She had given him everything, her heart, her trust, her love, and he had taken it all, slowly wearing down her spirit with each lie and every broken promise.

And now, here she was. She had let him pull her into this darkness, had allowed him to make her feel like she wasn't enough, like she wasn't worthy of the love and commitment she longed for.

But the worst part was that she still loved him. She had been so afraid of being alone that she let him stay, let him convince her that this was love, that the chaos, the emotional rollercoaster, was worth the fleeting moments of affection.

After that night, Seven retreated into herself. The shame she felt was suffocating. She had never been the kind of person to lose control, to let someone break her in such a way. But Michael had always had this ability to do just that. He was a master at making her feel small, at making her believe she was the problem when, in reality, it was him all along.

Her mind often drifted back to that moment, the knife in her hand, the emptiness in her chest. She couldn't forget the way she felt, like she was suffocating, drowning in her own emotions, desperate to make him understand. But he never did. Michael always deflected, always made it about something else, never once taking responsibility for the damage he had caused.

And so Seven was left to pick up the pieces, to try to piece herself back together after he had shattered her. The pain of that night lingered long after the fight had ended, and she hated herself for letting him get that far under her skin.

The Push and Pull

Despite everything, Michael always came back. And Seven always let him. She hated herself for it, hated the power he had over her. But each time he reached out, whether it was a simple "Hey, thinking about you" or an unexpected visit, her heart betrayed her.

Her friends didn't understand. "Why do you keep letting him hurt you?" they would ask, their voices laced with frustration.

She didn't have an answer. She wanted to believe it was because she loved him, because their bond was too strong to sever. But deep down, she knew it was fear—the fear of being alone, the fear of starting over, the fear that no one else would ever understand her the way Michael did.

There were times when Michael's words revealed a depth that caught Seven completely off guard. He wasn't as clueless or emotionally stunted as he often pretended to be. The truth was, Michael saw things, and felt things, more clearly than he let on. And one conversation in particular stayed with her, a moment when his insight had felt like a punch to the gut.

It was late one night, after one of their usual cycles of breaking apart and then finding their way back to each other. They were lying on the couch in her living room, Ryan asleep in the next room. The air was heavy, a mix of exhaustion and unspoken truths.

Michael was staring at the ceiling, his hands resting on his stomach, when he broke the silence.

"You ever seen Hancock?" he asked out of nowhere.

Seven blinked, confused by the sudden shift in topic. "The superhero movie? Yeah, a long time ago. Why?"

He turned his head to look at her, his gaze steady and uncharacteristically serious. "You remember how Hancock and Mary are drawn to each other? How they can't stay away no matter what they do?"

Seven's heart skipped a beat. She sat up slightly, her pulse quickening. "Yeah, I remember," she said cautiously.

Michael sat up too, running a hand through his hair. "That's us, Sev," he said, his voice low but charged with emotion. "We're like them. Two pieces of the same damn thing. And every time we try to be close, it's like the world tries to tear us apart."

Seven stared at him, the weight of his words sinking in. She had always felt the intensity of their connection, the way it seemed to defy logic. But hearing him articulate it so plainly, so vulnerably, shook her.

"Michael..." she began, her voice trembling.

He cut her off, shaking his head. "I know I've messed up. I know I don't deserve you half the time. But don't act like you don't feel it too. Don't act like this thing between us isn't bigger than either of us."

She opened her mouth to respond, but no words came out. Because he was right. As much as she wanted to deny it, as much as she wanted to dismiss their connection as something fleeting or toxic, she couldn't. What they had was real, raw, and overwhelming at times, even unbearable.

And for him to make that comparison, to reference Hancock of all things, made her realize something she hadn't fully acknowledged before: Michael wasn't as clueless as he often seemed. He knew. He had always known, just like she had.

In the days and weeks that followed, Seven couldn't stop thinking about that conversation. She replayed it in her mind, dissecting every word, every look. Michael had seen through her walls, through the defenses she had spent years building, and he had named the very thing she was too afraid to confront.

The Hancock comparison was ridiculous and profound all at once. The idea of being spiritually tethered to someone, of being bound in a way that defied logic or reason, resonated with her deeply. It was both a comfort and a curse.

Seven found herself reading about the concept of soulmates, about karmic bonds and spiritual contracts. She didn't believe in those things, not fully, but the descriptions felt too familiar to dismiss. Relationships like hers and Michael's weren't meant to be easy. These types of relation-ships were meant to teach, to challenge, to break and rebuild.

One evening, as she sat on her porch watching the sunset, Seven thought back to all the times she had tried to walk away from Michael. Each time, the universe had seemed to conspire to bring them back together. A chance meeting at the grocery store. A song on the radio that reminded her of him. A dream that left her waking up in tears, his name on her lips.

It was like they were two magnets, unable to resist the pull, no matter how hard they tried.

And yet, as much as she felt tethered to him, Seven couldn't ignore the pain that came with their connection. Was it worth it? she wondered. Was the depth of their bond enough to justify the heartache it brought?

She didn't have an answer. But for the first time, she allowed herself to consider the possibility that Michael wasn't just a chapter in her story, he was part of the thread that wove the whole thing together.

Months later, during one of their quieter moments, Seven brought it up again.

"You really believe what you said?" she asked, her voice tentative. "About us being like Hancock and Mary?"

Michael looked at her, his expression softening. "Yeah," he said simply. "I do. Don't you?"

Seven hesitated, then nodded. "I guess I do."

He reached for her hand, lacing his fingers with hers. "We're not perfect, Sev. We're probably gonna mess this up a hundred more times. But whatever this is, it's real. And I'm not gonna let it go."

His words lingered in the air, heavy with promise and uncertainty. And for the first time in a long time, Seven allowed herself to believe that maybe, just maybe, they were meant to figure it out together.

The Weight of It All

As Seven sat alone in her kitchen, the memories of Michael and Rowan swirling in her mind, she felt the weight of it all pressing down on her. The love she had given, the pain she had endured, the years she had spent trying to be enough for men who couldn't see her worth, it was almost too much to bear.

But in the midst of the darkness, there was a flicker of light. Ryan. Her daughter was her reason, her anchor. She had to be strong, not just for herself, but for the little girl who depended on her.

Seven took a deep breath, the resolve settling in her chest like a solid weight. She couldn't change the past, couldn't undo the mistakes she had made or the pain she had endured. But she could take control of her future.

"This is my life," she whispered, her voice steady and firm. "And I'm taking it back.

4

Echo's of the Past

Seven sat alone in the dimly lit kitchen, the remnants of a glass of wine still lingering on the counter. She had long since stopped drinking to numb the pain. Now, it felt more like an old habit, an attempt to fill the void that seemed to stretch endlessly in her life. Her fingers traced the edge of the journal in front of her, with her mind far away from the present.

Memories of Brad flooded her thoughts, and she couldn't help but reflect on how different everything could have been if she had made different choices. The echoes of the past haunted her, reverberating with every passing moment. She thought of the man who had loved her so deeply, who had treated her like royalty. Brad had given her everything; his time, his love, and his unwavering devotion. But she had turned him away.

She was consumed with fear.

She feared commitment, the loss of freedom, and the possibility of failing him, even though all he had ever wanted was her heart. The choice

Seven made years ago now felt like an unbearable weight, heavier with time.

"Why did I let him go?" she whispered to herself, a question she had asked a thousand times. The pain of regret settled into her chest, tight and suffocating. If she had just said yes, if she had let go of the ghosts of the past, maybe she could have built the life Brad had so desperately wanted to share with her.

But no. She hesitated, uncertain about the future, wary of the expectations and responsibilities that loomed ahead. She feared making a choice that might one day feel more like confinement than freedom.

Brad was the one man who truly saw her, the one who never tried to change her or mold her into someone else. He loved her exactly as she was and demonstrated it every single day. Steady and dependable, he would have given her the world. Yet, when it came time to choose, Seven hesitated. Fear held her back, and she let him slip away.

Brad's Unwavering Love

Brad had loved Seven with a devotion she had never experienced before. He was the kind of man who went above and beyond to make her feel special. He didn't just treat her like a queen, he treated her like his partner, his equal, his confidante. He would cook for her after long days, always preparing her favorite meals, and clean the apartment when she was too exhausted. He would chauffeur her and her friends to clubs, treating them all with kindness and respect, offering whatever he could to make them feel at ease. Brad gave her the world in small gestures, showing her that he loved her not just in words, but in actions. Not only did her friends love him, but Seven's family adored Brad, too. He had them all wrapped around his finger, effortlessly.

Seven had never doubted Brad's love. It wasn't the kind of love that required grand declarations or extravagant gestures; it was steady, dependable, and real. He loved her with consistency, and that made it all the more meaningful. When they argued, as all couples did, Brad was the first to apologize. He didn't hold grudges or let things fester. He was quick to listen, to understand her perspective, even when she couldn't fully understand her own.

But despite all of that, Seven found herself stuck. She had spent so much time waiting for Michael to change, waiting for him to commit, that she couldn't fully give herself to Brad. Every time he tried to take their relationship to the next level, Seven would retreat. The fear of commitment, of facing the unknown, blocked her from embracing the life Brad was offering.

One evening, as they were watching a movie together, the storyline struck a chord with Seven. It was about a man who left his wife when she became seriously ill. A wave of sadness for the woman in the story washed over her, and it also brought up her own insecurities and fears about the future. Seven stopped the film and turned to Brad, her heart heavy with unspoken questions.

"If that happened to me," she said, her voice trembling slightly, "or something even worse, would you leave me or hesitate to stay? You can be honest, Brad."

Brad didn't hesitate. He looked at her with all the sincerity in his eyes, the love so clear in his gaze. "Absolutely not," he replied, his voice steady and full of conviction. "I love you so much. I don't care about that. As long as I'm with you, as your husband, I'll be there. Through sickness and in health, you have my word."

Seven's heart fluttered, warmth spreading through her chest. "Babe," she whispered, her eyes filled with gratitude and love. "That's so sweet, and I believe you."

They kissed, lingering in the moment. Brad's unwavering love filled her with a deep sense of peace. But even as they continued the movie, Seven was compelled to contemplate the vulnerability she was avoiding. She was always fearful of complete devotion, not only due to her history but also from a dread of disappointment. Yet here was Brad—solid, steadfast, and completely willing to stand by her no matter what.

Seven inevitably wondered about why she always seemed to hold back. Why did she say no to his proposal of marriage? Why did she let the fear of commitment overshadow the love right in front of her?

Brad desired marriage, a family, a future with her. When he asked her to marry him, she said no.

"I'm not ready," she said, her voice filled with hesitation. "I need time."

Deep down, she knew the truth, even if she wasn't ready to face it. She hadn't been ready because part of her was still holding on to the hope that Michael, her first love, the man who always kept her at arm's length, might finally change. She clung to the possibility that he would choose her, choose commitment, and claim her as his partner at last.

But Brad, with his steady and unwavering love, waited patiently, hoping she would realize he was the one who could give her everything she needed. However, she still clung to Michael. Maintaining the hope that Michael might soon come to his senses. It seemed easier than embracing the uncertainty of a future with Brad.

Her hesitations led to a deep sense of regret. Brad was ready, but she was unable to meet him there. The love he offered was real and tangible, but she was too frightened to accept it.

In the quiet of her kitchen, Seven reflected on the choice she made and the life she might have lived with Brad. It was a life filled with stability, love, and commitment, everything she always wanted. But she remained too afraid to let go of the past, too afraid to take the leap. And now, Brad was married to someone else, someone who was willing to take that step with him. And Seven was left with the lingering sense that she let something beautiful slip through her fingers.

The days passed, but the regret never fully left her. She couldn't stop thinking about what she lost, about the man who loved her with an open heart, who did everything in his power to make her happy. Brad deserved more than what she'd given him. And now, all she could do was wonder about the life they might have shared together.

Seven would never forget the day she and Brad went to church together, just before everything began to unravel. He drove up from the military base to join her for Sunday service, a small gesture, but one that carried a weight she did not fully realize at the time. It wasn't just the effort of the drive, or the simple act of being there. It was the depth of his commitment, the love behind it, that made it feel sacred. This wasn't a place they'd frequented together. Seven attended once before, invited by a friend, but Brad never set foot in that church.

It was in that unfamiliar space, amidst strangers and prayers, that the unexpected happened. During the sermon, the pastor, who knew nothing of their story, paused mid-sentence, his eyes scanning the room before landing directly on them. Without warning, he spoke, his words sharp and direct, cutting through the air like a divine interruption.

"Seven," the pastor's voice rang out, clear and unwavering. "You have a man beside you who loves you deeply, a man who would be good for you. Brad could be your strength if you let go of your past, if you take that leap of faith. But if you refuse, he will move on. And you will regret it."

Seven's heart stuttered in her chest. The room seemed to close in around her, the walls pressing inward as every eye turned toward her. It was as if the universe itself had paused in that moment, the weight of the pastor's words settling over her like a heavy cloak. Her breath caught, her mind scrambled to make sense of what was happening. Brad's hand, warm and steady, tightened around hers, his eyes locked on hers, waiting, hoping for something she was unwilling to give.

Every word of the pastor's prophecy pierced through her, a stark and undeniable truth she was unable to escape. It felt like a warning, but also an invitation, a call to step into something real, something new.

The truth was too much to face. She was still holding on to the fragments of her past, the unspoken hope that maybe, just maybe, Michael would change. The bond she shared with him, though frayed and distant, was still there, pulsing just beneath the surface. It was a connection that had long ago become her comfort, the thing that anchored her, even when she knew it wasn't healthy. And Brad? Brad was everything she needed, loving, patient, devoted. He was everything she had prayed for in so many ways. But in that moment, she was blind to it.

Brad was hopeful. His eyes shone with the possibility of a future, a future he believed in, with her by his side. But for Seven, the fear was overwhelming. Was she able to let go of the life she had known, the hopes and dreams she once placed on Michael, to build something new with Brad? She questioned whether this love, this man, was destined for her.

In that fleeting moment, when everything hung in the balance, she failed him. And the moment she saw the hurt in Brad's eyes, the quiet disappointment that was evident, she knew. She knew she made the wrong choice.

The words of the pastor echoed in her mind long after they left the church, the weight of them pressing against her chest, relentless. *You may regret it.* And in that moment, Seven understood. The past had a grip on her, but so did Brad's love. And now she lost both.

The Breakup

In the weeks that followed, Brad's patience wore thin. He was waiting for Seven to reconcile with her feelings, but when she couldn't promise a future with him, he gave her an ultimatum.

"I need more than this, Seven," he said, his voice tight with frustration. "I need a higher level of commitment. If you can't give me that, then I can't keep doing this."

Seven broke up with him soon after. She couldn't ask him to wait forever. She didn't want to force him into a life of uncertainty. But deep down, she knew she needed to release him, and she knew that he deserved better.

And so Brad moved on. He met someone else, someone who didn't hesitate to give him what he wanted. He married her, started a family, and built a life. The life Seven was too scared to give him.

The Regret

Seven thought back to the day she heard about Brad's marriage. A mutual friend called her, the news breaking through the fog of her own life like a sharp gust of wind. Brad found happiness with someone else. It wasn't just that he moved on; it was the realization that he found someone who could give him what he always wanted with Seven, a future, a commitment, a family, and love without hesitation.

Seven felt the weight of her choice. The regret was like a boulder sitting on her chest, and she was unable to escape. She let him go. And now he was happy without her.

She often found herself thinking of him. Did he ever look back? Did he regret walking away? Seven wanted to believe he'd found the happiness he deserved, but a part of her would always wonder: What if?

The Self-Reflection

Seven stood by the window, a glass of wine in her hand, watching the last rays of sunlight fade into the evening. The reflection of her own face stared back at her from the darkened glass, a reminder of the choices she made, and the ones she hadn't.

Her failure to commit cost her far more than just Brad. It wasn't the first time she sabotaged something real, something that could've been everything she needed. She lost the chance to build a life with someone who loved her unconditionally. She lost the future she could've had, family, stability, the love Brad had offered so freely, without hesitation.

For so long, she waited for someone who would never be able to give her what she needed. Years wasted, hoping Michael might change, waiting for him to return. But in doing so, she pushed away the very thing that could've brought her the happiness she'd longed for. Now, she was left with nothing but the empty space where Brad once was, everything she ever wanted slipping away.

The realization hit her hard: her fear of commitment wasn't just a shield. It was a prison. Whenever love presented itself, she withdrew, believing total commitment to someone else would leave her entrapped, in a destiny lacking Michael. However, Michael never returned, not in a way that she expected, and she was left with nothing but the weight of her own indecision.

Seven took a deep breath and set the glass down, the sharp edge of regret cutting through her. She reached for her journal, the pages waiting for her to pour out the thoughts that were circling in her mind. She didn't know what the future held, but she knew one thing for certain: she couldn't keep clinging to the past.

She needed to forgive herself for the mistakes she made, for the chances she let slip away, and for the fear that kept her from fully embracing the love she deserved.

It wasn't too late to start again. She was still alive, still breathing, still capable of creating the life she always dreamed of. And maybe, just maybe, she could finally let go of the past and begin to rebuild her future.

5

Distant Memories

Amid everything, the past calls to Seven in moments she least expects it, when she's folding laundry, waiting at a red light, or sipping her morning coffee. It isn't just a whisper; it's a symphony, pulling her back to a time when life was colorful and unburdened, a canvas painted with laughter, love and the kind of magic only childhood could create.

Family gatherings were the brightest strokes on that canvas. They were sprawling events, effortlessly orchestrated, but full of life and chaos. Each gathering felt larger than life, a celebration that seemed to defy the rules of time and space, where every family member, immediate and extended, found a place at the table. These memories weren't just moments; they were entire worlds Seven could step into, worlds that felt so real she could almost touch them.

Arrival: The Promise of Joy

Every family gathering began with the same sacred ritual, an unspoken choreography that never seemed to change no matter how many years passed. As the family car cruised down the familiar gravel road leading to her aunt's house, Seven felt an electric thrill course through her veins. Even as a child, she knew this was more than just a visit; it was a homecoming.

Her aunt's' home stood like a sentinel of time, its white shutters slightly crooked but endlessly endearing, as though they were winking in quiet welcome. The wraparound porch, adorned with hanging ferns and her aunt's favorite wind chime, seemed to radiate warmth even before anyone stepped onto its creaky wooden planks.

Inside the car, the air was alive with anticipation. Seven and her siblings would fidget in their seats, their energy barely contained. "How much longer?" one of them would ask, for the fifth time that hour, as if the answer would magically shorten the journey. Seven's mother would sigh in mock exasperation, but even she couldn't hide her smile.

As they turned into the driveway, the familiar scene unfolded like the first act of a beloved play. Cousins spilled out of the house like characters eager for their cue, their laughter already filling the air. Seven pressed her face to the window, her breath fogging the glass, trying to take it all in at once. The house, the yard, the people—it was a tableau of joy, a frozen moment that felt eternal.

The car came to a stop, and for a brief second, the world seemed to pause. Seven's father hadn't even shifted into park before she flung open the door, her shoes barely touching the ground before she was running toward the laughter.

"Wait! Don't forget to--" her mother started, but Seven was already gone, her heart leading her before her head could catch up.

A World of First Impressions

Each arrival felt like a miniature adventure. As soon as Seven's feet hit the gravel, a sensory symphony unfolded around her. Warm, smoky aromas from the grill mingled with the tang of lemonade being stirred in oversized pitchers. Crickets chirped in the background, creating a lazy soundtrack to the chaos of children's laughter and the soft murmur of adults exchanging greetings.

Her youngest cousins were already darting across the yard, their legs a blur as they chased each other in a game that had no clear rules but seemed endlessly fun. "Seven!" one of them called, his face lighting up at the sight of her. "You're finally here!"

Before she could respond, her older cousins were at her side, tugging her toward the house. "Come on," they urged, their voices overlapping. "We have to show you something!"

Inside, the house was a world unto itself. Seven could hear the distant clatter of dishes in the kitchen, her aunt's commanding voice rising above the din. "Who left the butter out? It's melting!" Meanwhile, the living room was already alive with music, her uncles tuning the karaoke machine as if preparing for a concert.

The Sacred Porch Ritual

But before Seven could dive into the chaos, there was one important ritual to complete. The porch was a liminal space, a bridge between the outside world and the sanctuary of family. Her aunt and uncle stood there, waiting to greet each new arrival like sentinels of love and tradition.

Her uncle's hug was the kind that wrapped around you twice, his laughter rumbling in his chest as he exclaimed, "Look at you! Taller every time I see you!" Her aunt, always a mix of sternness and softness, would press a kiss to her cheek, her hands lingering on Seven's shoulders as if to confirm she was undoubtedly there.

These moments were brief but grounding, a quiet acknowledgment that no matter how far life pulled them apart, this was a place they all returned to.

The Energy of Reconnection

As soon as Seven crossed the threshold into the house, it was as though a spell was cast. She felt lighter, freer, as if the burdens of the outside world couldn't follow her here. Time moved differently in this place; hours felt like minutes, and joy came in waves, not moments.

Seven had not seen most of her cousins since the last family gathering, and as they exchanged familiar glances, it felt as though no time had passed. The bond between them had always been effortlessly strong, a connection that picked up where it left off, no matter the months or years between their meetings.

"Remember that time when Seven convinced all of us she could drive?" Jake said, grinning as he leaned back in his chair.

The mention of the story brought an immediate wave of laughter, as if they had all been waiting for it.

"Yeah, I still don't know how she got us all to believe it," Mara added with a chuckle. "She must've been what—ten? Twelve?"

"Ten, maybe?" Seven said, rolling her eyes as she shook her head at herself. "I was just trying to look cool, you know?"

The group laughed harder; the memory coming to life in a way that felt just as ridiculous now as it had back then.

"We were all at Nick's house, and we were playing in his car," Jake said, almost too eager to dive into the details. "You were the one who jumped in the driver's seat first, Seven. You said you could drive, and we all just went along with it! Like, why would we ever think that was a good idea?"

Seven laughed at how easily they'd all bought into her plan, how they'd trusted her with their safety despite her clear lack of driving skills.

"I didn't think it would actually roll," Seven admitted, her voice filled with mock regret. "I was just trying to be the cool older cousin, showing off."

The group erupted in laughter again, remembering how Seven had confidently put the car in neutral. The next thing they knew, the car had rolled, gradually at first, then gaining speed.

"Then the car started moving, and it was like everything froze for a second," Mara said, shaking her head. "All of us started freaking out, screaming at you to stop, but you were just sitting there, frozen too, looking like you had no clue what was happening."

Seven smiled sheepishly. "What was I supposed to do? I thought I was just pushing a button or something. Next thing I knew, we were rolling down the driveway."

"Yeah, rolling right toward the street!" Kase, Seven's younger brother, added, laughing as he recalled how they'd all panicked in that moment. "We were all screaming, thinking we were about to crash Nick's car, and I was sure we were all going to die."

"And then thank God for Nick," Mara said, smiling fondly at the memory. "I don't know how he did it, but he came running out of the house and jumped through the window to stop the car. I swear, it was like he saved all our lives in that moment."

Seven grinned, her heart warming at the thought of her older cousin's quick thinking. "I'll never forget how he pulled me out of the seat like I was a rag doll, and he got in, took the car out of neutral, and stopped it. It was the craziest thing I'd ever seen."

"And the funniest part was, we all thought we were going to get grounded, but Nick just laughed and told us never to do that again," Kase added, still laughing at how they all had to pretend it wasn't as bad as it felt.

Seven laughed, shaking her head. "I'll never live that one down, will I?"

"Nope," Mara said, smiling widely. "But at least we can laugh about it now."

The memory, once a source of embarrassment for Seven, had now turned into one of those family stories that only grew funnier with age. They all laughed together, the sound carrying into the evening, echoing with the joy of shared history and the bond they would always carry with them, no matter how much time passed.

The Promise of Something Eternal

What struck Seven most about these arrivals wasn't just the joy, they were a promise, a quiet reassurance that no matter how much the world changed, some things stayed the same. This house, this family, this feeling of belonging; it was a constant in an ever-shifting world.

And though Seven didn't have the words for it then, she felt the weight of that promise in her heart. It was a thread that connected her to something larger than herself, something sacred.

As the evening unfolded and the rituals of games, food, and laughter began, Seven would pause every so often to take it all in. These moments, these people, this place, it was magic. And even as a child, she knew she would carry it with her always.

The Games: Childhood in Motion

The games were endless. Tag was always the first, a chaotic free-for-all that sprawled across the yard and beyond. Seven loved feeling the wind rushing past her face, her heart pounding in her chest as she dodged and darted, her laughter mingling with the shouts of her cousins. The yard was their kingdom, the trees their hiding spots, the porch their safe zone.

Then came the races. Someone would draw a starting line in the dirt, and the kids would line up shoulder to shoulder, their sneakers digging into the grass. Seven was always the fastest—faster than the boys, without a doubt. She'd run like there was no tomorrow, legs pumping furiously, arms swinging wildly, eyes locked on the makeshift finish line ahead. The adults would cheer from the sidelines, their voices rising over the yard, urging them on. And every time, Seven would cross the line first, sparing no humility as she raised her arms in victory. The boys would lower their heads, shaking them in disbelief, while Seven celebrated, basking in her win without an ounce of hesitation.

Inside, quieter games took place. The younger kids crowded around board games, their faces serious as they rolled dice or moved game pieces, while the older cousins claimed a corner for card games. Seven always found herself torn between the two worlds, her curiosity pulling her back and forth as she tried to soak up everything.

The Kitchen: The Heart of the Gathering

The kitchen was a world unto itself, a place of warmth and delicious chaos. Seven loved sneaking in, drawn by the aromas wafting through the air. Her aunt was always at the center of it all, moving between the stove and the counter with practiced ease. Her aunts worked around her, chopping vegetables, stirring pots, and taste-testing with a level of precision that Seven found fascinating.

"Seven, don't just stand there, hand me that bowl," her aunt would say, her tone stern but her eyes twinkling. Seven would spring into action, eager to be part of the magic.

The food was a feast for the senses: roasted meats glistening with juices, casseroles bubbling with cheese, salads fresh and vibrant, and desserts that seemed almost too beautiful to eat. Seven's favorite was always the strawberry cheesecake, its velvety cream filling topped with glistening red berries. She'd sneak a bite whenever she could, giggling as her aunt playfully swatted her hand away with a wooden spoon.

The living room was more than just a room, it was the heartbeat of every family gathering, a stage where joy and laughter took center stage. At its heart was the karaoke machine, an ancient but revered piece of technology that had seen decades of use. Years of use had worn its buttons smooth and frayed its microphone cord, yet it held an unquestioned magic.

When the adults took the stage, the room transformed. Seven's uncles always led the charge, their performances a mix of genuine talent and over-the-top theatrics. Uncle Marvin was the crooner, his deep baritone giving life to love ballads that made the older aunts swoon and the younger ones roll their eyes with affectionate laughter. He closed his eyes as he sang, one hand on his heart, as if he were serenading the entire family.

Meanwhile, Uncle Stan played the part of the clown, turning every performance into a spectacle. He would strut around the room, twirling an imaginary cane, and strike dramatic poses that had the kids doubled over in laughter. "Encore! Encore!" they'd shout, and Stan would oblige with an exaggerated bow before launching into another act.

Aunt Paula was the wild card. With her unshakeable confidence and a flair for the dramatic, she'd belt out power ballads that shook the room, flipping her hair and pointing to the "audience" as though she were performing at Madison Square Garden. Her daughters would cringe and cheer in equal measure, and someone would inevitably yell, "Go, Mom!"

A Children's Revolution

For the kids, the living room was a world of possibility. The moment the adults vacated the "stage," the children swarmed it like a pack of performers eager for their moment in the spotlight. Seven's cousins jockeyed for the microphone, each claiming their turn with the bravado only kids could muster.

Seven always hesitated, hovering near the back of the crowd, until one of her cousins shoved the microphone into her hands. "Your turn!" they'd say, grinning mischievously. The familiar thrill of nervous excitement coursed through her as she stood before her family, her small frame dwarfed by the crowd of eager faces watching her.

She chose her go-to song, a cheerful pop anthem that always got everyone clapping along. The first few notes were shaky, her voice faltering as she tried to find her courage. But then, as her cousins cheered her on, something shifted. Seven let go of her self-consciousness and sang with abandon, her voice growing louder and stronger with every word.

The adults joined in, clapping in time to the beat, their smiles warm and encouraging. By the time she hit the chorus, the entire room was singing with her, their voices blending into a joyful cacophony. Seven felt a rush of exhilaration, her cheeks flushed and her heart racing.

Dance Floor Dreams

Once the singing subsided, the living room morphed into a dance floor. Someone turned up the music, and the kids spilled into the open space, their limbs flailing in wild abandon. Seven was right in the middle of it all, her arms swinging and her feet stomping in a rhythm that was uniquely her own.

The adults served as impromptu judges, their voices rising above the music as they shouted scores and handed out candy prizes. "Ten out of ten for energy!" her uncle declared as Seven spun in dizzying circles.

Seven didn't care about the scores or the prizes—it was the freedom she craved. The freedom to move, to laugh, to be seen and celebrated. Her cousins cheered her on, and for a moment, she felt like a star in her own little universe.

A Stage of Connection

The living room wasn't just a space for games and music—it was a place of connection. It was where family members, young and old, came together to celebrate each other's quirks and talents. Seven's uncle, typically reserved, surprised everyone by stepping up to the microphone one year to sing a traditional folk song. His voice cracked with emotion as he sang, and the room fell silent. Everyone captivated by the raw beauty of the moment.

Even the youngest members of the family got their time to shine. Seven's little brother, barely five years old, was coaxed into singing a nursery rhyme. His tiny, hesitant voice drew applause that rivaled the loudest cheers of the night. Seven beamed with pride as he giggled and ducked his head, his joy infectious.

Memories Etched in Time

As the evening wore on, the living room became a kaleidoscope of memories. Seven would later remember the way the light from the chandelier caught in her cousins' hair as they danced, the sound of her uncle's hearty laughter echoing off the walls, and the warmth of her aunt's smile as she clapped along to the music.

These moments weren't just entertainment, they were the threads that wove their family together. And even as the years passed and life took them in different directions, the living room remained a touchstone, a reminder of the joy and connection they shared.

For Seven, it wasn't just a stage, it was a sanctuary. A place where she felt seen, loved, and celebrated. And as she danced and sang with her family, she knew that these were the moments she would carry with her forever.

The Raffle: The Thrill of Possibility

The raffle was always the highlight of the evening. Each ticket felt like a golden opportunity, and Seven clutched hers tightly, her fingers crinkling the edges as she waited for the numbers to be called.

"Four... seven... two... three... six!"

Seven's heart raced as she checked her ticket, hoping against hope that she held the winning number. When she didn't win, she felt a brief pang of disappointment, but the excitement of watching her little brother leap into the air instantly replaced it. His ticket raised high as he claimed his prize.

The Evening Glow: A World of Magic

As the sun dipped below the horizon, the yard transformed. String lights flickered to life, casting a warm glow over the scene. The music softened, blending with the sounds of the night, crickets chirping, the rustle of leaves in the breeze, and occasional bursts of laughter from the adults.

The evening's magic truly began when the fireflies appeared, their tiny lights dancing like nature's response to the string of lights overhead. Seven's little brother was the first to spot them, his excited shout capturing everyone's attention. In no time, the younger kids were darting across the yard, jars in hand, chasing the glowing insects with gleeful determination.

"Be gentle!" someone called, their voice tinged with the wisdom of age. "Don't hurt them."

Seven watched as her brother cupped his hands around a firefly, his face glowing with wonder as the tiny creature blinked on and off. She joined him, the cool grass tickling her toes as she crouched to help him transfer his prize into a jar. They held the jar up to the light, marveling at the miniature galaxy they had created.

Seven loved this time of day, when the chaos of the afternoon gave way to a quieter, more intimate atmosphere. She would sit on the porch swing, her legs dangling, and watch as the world around her seemed to settle into a gentle rhythm.

The adults gathered around the patio tables, shuffling cards and exchanging playful banter that rose and fell like a familiar melody. Seven's eldest cousin, her mother's beloved nephew, was the loudest of them all, his booming laughter ringing out with every victory or teasing remark. Her mother watched him with a fond, knowing smile, shaking her head as if she had long ago embraced his larger-than-life personality as part of the family's charm.

Reflections: The Weight of Memory

As the night wore on and the voices grew softer, Seven felt a quiet peace settle over her. She thought about how these moments, so simple and fleeting, seemed to hold a kind of sacredness. The laughter, the stories, the shared meals—they were all pieces of a larger tapestry, one woven with love and connection.

She leaned back in the swing, her gaze drifting to the stars that now glittered brightly overhead. The fireflies had faded into the darkness, their brief dance over, but their memory lingered like the warmth of a hug.

Beneath the soft glow of string lights and surrounded by the familiar hum of her family's voices, Seven felt an unshakable sense of belonging. These moments weren't just memories; they were imprints on her heart, as permanent and timeless as the stars above. No matter where life took her or how far she strayed, she knew she would carry this feeling with her, a guiding light, always leading her back home.

Looking back, Seven often wonders how life could have felt so perfect. How could everything have seemed so easy, so carefree? She now knows that perfection was an illusion, a deliberately constructed facade that shielded her from the complexities of adult life.

If there were family tensions, she never felt them. If there were secrets, they were masked so well that even the adults seemed to forget them, at least for a day. The older generations had mastered the art of pretending, of creating a world where love and laughter masked whatever cracks might have existed beneath the surface.

And yet, even with the knowledge of hindsight, Seven holds onto these memories. More than just fragments of her past, they are symbolic of so much more. Such memories bring back a time of an unbreakable world, love acting as a shield against negativity, and happiness being as easy as a warm embrace or shared laughter.

These memories are her anchor, her proof that life can be beautiful even when it's messy and complicated. In her quiet moments, she returns to them, letting herself relive the joy, the connection, and the love that filled those days.

For Seven, these memories are not just a part of her past; they are a part of her soul. And no matter how far she drifts from that world, she knows she will always carry it with her, a light that shines even in the darkest moments.

6

Family Ties

The warmth that had once wrapped itself around Seven's memories began to cool as the years passed. What she had once seen as a tapestry of unconditional love and connection started to fray at the edges. The cracks were subtle at first—mere whispers of something deeper, something darker, lurking beneath the surface of the family she had idolized.

Seven had always been close to her cousins. They weren't just family; they were her best friends, her confidants, her partners in adventure. The bond they shared felt unshakable, forged in the fires of childhood joy and innocence. They were more like siblings than cousins, and in those early years, Seven couldn't imagine her life without them. But as she grew older, her perspective shifted.

The Masks Begin to Slip

Seven's family had always been a mix of personalities, and she had loved them all fiercely. Her aunts and uncles, her cousins, even the distant relatives who showed up sporadically; they were all part of the vibrant, chaotic world she called home. Yet, as she matured, she noticed things she hadn't before.

There was an unspoken tension she couldn't fully define but felt deeply, an undercurrent that simmered just beneath the surface. It wasn't obvious at first, showing itself only in fleeting sidelong glances or offhand remarks disguised as jokes, remarks that carried a subtle edge, cutting just enough to leave her uneasy.

"Must be nice, huh? One cousin commented, eyeing Seven's new bike with a smile that didn't quite reach their eyes. Seven didn't understand it then, but she remembered the way the words made her feel, like she had done something wrong simply by having something they didn't.

Seven's mother, Trisha, had worked tirelessly to give her children a life filled with opportunities and comforts. Even with the absence of Seven's biological father, Trisha had built a world where her children never wanted for anything. Each sibling had their own room, their own space, their own sense of individuality nurtured by a mother who refused to let their circumstances define them.

This presented a stark contrast to the lives of some of their family members, who seemed perpetually stuck in cycles of co-dependence and stagnation. Seven didn't think much of it at first; she loved her family too much to let those differences matter. But the differences began to matter to them.

The Unfolding Truth

As the years went on, the dynamics shifted. Seven's family seemed to gain more stability, more success, and with it came a subtle but undeniable change in how they were treated. Family members who had once been warm and welcoming now seemed guarded, even resentful.

Trisha, perpetually optimistic, chose not to see it. She opened her home to anyone who needed it, her heart too big and her boundaries too soft. For years, she had gone above and beyond for her family, not just out of love but, Seven later realized, out of a deep need to be accepted. Trisha's childhood had been fraught with its own struggles, and her way of healing seemed to be pouring herself into the people she believed would never leave her behind.

At first, Seven considered it amazing. Having relatives live with them felt like an extended sleepover, a chance to strengthen the bonds that already felt so unbreakable. She loved the commotion, the late-night talks, and the sense of togetherness that seemed to fill the house.

But the excitement quickly faded as the reality set in.

Those relatives who came to stay didn't just need shelter; they brought chaos. They made promises they didn't keep, took advantage of Trisha's generosity, and left behind messes, both literal and emotional, for someone else to clean up. Seven noticed the strain it put on her mother, the way Trisha tried to hide her exhaustion behind a forced smile.

Trisha seemed blind to the toll it was taking. She believed that if she kept giving her time, her money, her energy; she would finally be seen as indispensable, as someone worth cherishing. But Seven saw something her mother didn't: Trisha was feeding a never-ending hungry monster. No matter how much she gave, it was never enough. Her family didn't see her sacrifices as acts of love; they saw them as obligations she owed them.

Seven experienced a painful realization, one that tainted her view of the people she once admired.

The Shift in Seven

As Seven grew older, she recognized the same patterns playing out in her own relationships. Friends and family members who once felt like allies now seemed to take her kindness for granted. At first, she thought the problem might be her, that maybe she wasn't doing enough to keep them happy.

But with age came wisdom, and Seven saw through people in ways she hadn't before. She realized that her mother's approach, while rooted in love, lacked the boundaries necessary to foster genuine respect. Trisha's family didn't resent her generosity because they felt guilty for taking it, they resented it because it reminded them of their own inadequacies.

Seven, however, had boundaries. She proved unwilling to empty herself for others' validation, and the firmer her boundaries became, the clearer the true character of those surrounding her.

They didn't like it.

When Seven started saying "no," the warmth in their interactions cooled. Invitations dried up, phone calls left unanswered, and the family previously embracing her now seemed distant, even dismissive. At first, it hurt, but the more she reflected on her mother's experiences, the more Seven felt relieved.

She didn't want to spend her life running on the same treadmill as Trisha, chasing after the approval of people who would never truly value her.

Seeing Trisha with New Eyes

Seven's newfound clarity also changed how she saw her mother. She had always admired Trisha's strength and resilience, but now she saw the cracks beneath the surface. Trisha's endless giving wasn't just an act of love, it was also a way of trying to fill a void that couldn't be filled.

It broke Seven's heart to watch her mother pour so much of herself into people who seemed to take pleasure in draining her. Trisha would defend them, even when their actions were indefensible, saying things like, "They're family. We have to help them."

But Seven remained unconvinced.

"Helping someone doesn't mean letting them take advantage of you," Seven said one night during a heated argument. "You're not helping them grow, Mom. You're just making it easier for them to stay the same."

Trisha looked at her, stunned. It was one of the few times Seven had seen her mother at a loss for words.

"You don't understand," Trisha said, her voice softer now. "Family is everything. If we don't have that, what do we have?"

Seven stayed silent. She understood her mother's perspective, truly she did, but she couldn't ignore the truth. Trisha's idea of family wasn't built on love. It was held together by duty, a fragile bond masquerading as connection.

The Turning Point

The warmth Seven once enjoyed for her family cooled, replaced by a growing sense of disillusionment. These weren't the people she idolized in her childhood. They were flawed, selfish, and often cruel in ways she couldn't ignore.

But unlike Trisha, Seven was unwilling to sacrifice herself to keep the peace. She started pulling back, distancing herself from the family dynamics that once felt so comforting, but now felt suffocating. It wasn't easy, and it certainly wasn't without pain, but necessary.

Seven still loved her family, but she loved herself, too. And as she watched her mother continue to give and give and give, Seven vowed to do things differently.

She would help the people she loved, but she wouldn't let them take advantage of her. She would cherish the bonds that were genuine and let go of the ones that didn't serve her in a positive way.

Most importantly, she would hold on to her boundaries, no matter how much it hurt to enforce them. Because Seven learned something her mother didn't: love without respect wasn't love at all.

The Sibling Divide

It wasn't only her extended family that opened Seven's eyes; within her own household, a completely different dynamic was taking shape.

Kase, her brother, who was just a year younger, often seemed at odds with her. While Seven adored Kase for his larger than life personality and his ability to light up a room with his jokes and charisma, there was an underlying tension between them.

Seven couldn't wrap her mind around it. Kase drew people in with ease, his charm like a magnet, while she found herself on the outside looking in. Though others admired her looks, they often kept their distance, labeling her as unapproachable. Some even dismissed her as stuck-up and entitled, never bothering to see past the surface. If they had, they would have found someone fiercely loyal, quietly kind, and far deeper than they ever imagined.

Kase, however, always seemed to harbor a grievance when it came to Seven. "You get everything you want," he'd say, his tone cutting with barely disguised resentment. "Mom and Dad bend over backward for you, but they don't do half of that for me."

What Kase couldn't see was the complexity of Seven's relationship with Trisha. While their mother had a tendency to spoil her, there was an undercurrent of tension that often went unspoken. As Seven grew older, that strain only deepened, revealing a dynamic that was both tender and fraught. To Kase, it looked like blatant favoritism, a skewed balance where Seven always came out on top. But for Seven, it wasn't so simple. What Kase saw as privilege, she experienced as a love wrapped in complexities, silent battles, and expectations she didn't always know how to meet.

Despite his bitterness, Seven loved Kase deeply. She often defended him, even more than she did their youngest brother, Karter. But Kase made it difficult. He carried a chip on his shoulder, walking through life as if the world owed him something. He'd refuse invitations to hang out with Seven and Karter, then later accuse them of excluding him.

"Why don't you go with your favorite brother?" he'd say with a mocking tone, referring to Karter.

Seven and Karter shared a deep, unspoken bond, one built on mutual respect and understanding, something Kase never seemed interested in cultivating. To Karter, Seven was more than just a sibling; she was a role model, a steady source of guidance and support. But Kase saw her differently. To him, even her smallest achievements felt like a threat, and what he perceived as favoritism became an invisible battlefield, one where she did not know a competition even existed.

A New Lens

As Seven reflected on these dynamics, she saw patterns. Kase's bitterness wasn't about what he lacked, but about how he perceived the world around him. He seemed to resent the privileges they all shared, longing for a struggle that didn't exist in their suburban upbringing.

"You know we had a good childhood," Seven would remind him. "We didn't grow up in some urban drama or a music video. We had a stable home, excellent schools, everything we needed and more."

But Kase didn't want to hear it. He seemed determined to paint their upbringing as lacking, as if he needed an excuse for his feelings of alienation.

It pained Seven to feel the growing distance between them. She had always admired Kase in her own way, marveling at his effortless charm and ability to draw people in. But his constant scrutiny and tendency to find fault in her choices created a tension she couldn't quite understand.

Reflection: The Weight of Blood Ties

Family, Seven realized, was both a blessing and a burden. It was the source of her greatest joys and her deepest disappointments. It was a part of her, woven into the fabric of who she was, but it didn't have to define her.

Even with the tension between her and Kase, she couldn't bring herself to walk away completely. She still loved him, even if that love was complicated. But she knew she couldn't let their dysfunction dictate her life.

Seven still loved them all, but she no longer felt the need to hold on to the illusions of the past. She could cherish the wonderful memories while letting go of the pain. She could choose her own path, one that honored the love and strength her mother had given her while leaving behind the dysfunction that had shaped so much of her extended family.

In the end, Seven realized that family wasn't just about blood. It was about the people who showed up, the ones who stayed, and those who loved her unconditionally, not for what they could take, but simply because they cared. That, she decided, was the kind of family worth cherishing.

7

A Fragile Foundation

The days became longer and more burdensome, each one blurring into the next as Seven continued to navigate the tumultuous waters of her life. The moments of clarity she experienced while writing faded, eclipsed by the haze of wine and regret. Not that the wine solved anything, but it became a brief respite from a burdensome reality. It softened the edges of her thoughts, allowing her to slip into a world where everything wasn't so sharp, so painfully raw. But as she drank more, the fog grew thicker, and her guilt weighed heavier on her chest.

Ryan noticed the change. Seven could feel her daughter's gaze on her, even when she didn't have the strength to meet it. Ryan would ask in her small voice, "Mommy, can we play?" but Seven would often respond with a half-hearted "Maybe later," her mind wandering into places that didn't serve either of them. The once-vibrant little girl mirrored her mother's distance, the light in her eyes dimming with each passing day. Seven felt the guilt twist in her stomach, realizing the extent to which her emotional withdrawal affected her daughter. She hated Ryan was becoming more accustomed to her absence, despite her physical presence.

The strain in her relationship with her mother reappeared, too. Trisha's well-intentioned advice often seemed like a suffocating weight instead of the support Seven longed for. "You need to let go of this negativity," her mother told her one evening, her voice sharp with frustration. "You're letting people define your happiness. Focus on what's important: work, Ryan, and making a good life for yourself."

Seven heard those words countless times before, a refrain her mother often used to mask her own pain and sidestep the emotional voids she never confronted. It wasn't about her mother's ability to provide, she had ensured Seven never lacked for material comforts. However, provision did not constitute a connection. When it came to offering the emotional depth that made someone feel seen, valued, and understood, her mother would seem to lack.

Trisha's Emotional Disconnect

Seven's mind drifted to her childhood, to memories that should have been warm but always seemed cloaked in an unsettling chill. When she voiced her frustrations, her mother's eyes would glaze over, distant and impenetrable. "Why focus on the negatives?" Trisha would ask, her tone crisp, almost dismissive. Her words weren't a balm, they were armor, a way to sidestep the messy emotional truths Seven was trying to uncover. Trisha's shield was the same: an inventory of her sacrifices. The late nights. The tireless work. The roof over their heads. The food on their plates. But for Seven, all the tangible provisions in the world couldn't fill the emotional void between them. What good were warm meals and sturdy walls when the person meant to understand you most felt unreachable?

Trisha and Seven clashed often, their interactions bristling with unspoken tension. Seven's sharp tongue and fearless honesty seemed to unnerve her mother. She wasn't one to mince words; she called things as she saw them, not to wound but to reveal. Yet Trisha saw something more troubling in her daughter's strength. It signified more than defiance—it showed a true reflection of herself, unshackled from the self-imposed rules she'd held onto for so long. Seven's boldness challenged Trisha's tightly gripped control, a control she relied on to keep her world from unraveling. And that challenge wasn't welcome.

Trisha carried her strength like a badge, her pride rooted in her ability to hold everything together without so much as a crack in her facade. Yet Seven always seen the fissures, even as a child. She saw how her mother's fear of vulnerability seeped into their bond, weaving an invisible barrier neither of them surmounted. Trisha's world revolved around what could be measured—clean clothes, full bellies, solid shelter. But love? Love was something intangible, something Trisha unknowingly withheld. With every dismissal of her daughter's emotional needs, she added another brick to the towering wall between them.

Seven had tried, again and again, to bridge the distance. To say, in every way she knew how, that her mother's indifference cut her deeply. But Trisha's response never changed. "I don't know why you can't just be happy with what you have," she'd snap, the words sharp as glass. "You have it good you always have, Seven. Do you know how many people would kill for what you have, and would trade places with you?"

And there it was, their unresolvable dissonance. For Trisha, love was what could be provided, weighed, and counted. For Seven, love meant being seen, understood, and cherished. They spoke different languages, each one incomprehensible to the other. To Trisha, her sacrifices equated to gifts and all things material. To Seven, they felt like chains.

"I'm not ungrateful," Seven muttered to herself, her voice low, bitter. She stared into her glass, the deep red wine catching the light like a secret she couldn't share. With another pour, she let the liquid swirl and settle, hoping it would calm the ache in her chest. Each sip dulled the edge of her anger, but it could never smother the fire completely.

And yet, no matter how deep the divide between them, Seven had to believe her mother loved her. Not because of the sacrifices, not because of the lectures or the practicality of her care, but because love was the only thread tying them together. It was frayed, stretched thin by misunderstandings, but it was there, woven into the foundation of everything Trisha tried to build. Seven held onto that belief, even in the moments when the impact of their differences seemed overwhelming. Without it, the tightness in her chest would have been insurmountable.

This wasn't just frustration. It was a deep, bone-weary exhaustion. The endless cycle of trying to mend what seemed unfixable had worn her spirit thin. For all Trisha's strength, she never understood the power of vulnerability, of letting someone truly see her. That kind of emotion always seemed beyond her reach. And for Seven, it was the one thing she needed most.

Memories of a "Phone Father"

Seven's thoughts drifted to her father, Derek, the man who had always been more of an echo than a presence. He lived miles away, a distant figure who seemed to exist in the hazy periphery of her life. His calls were sporadic, his voice warm yet hollow, full of promises that dissolved like smoke. "I'll visit soon," he'd say, or, "Next time, we'll spend the entire weekend together." But "next time" never came. Derek was the father who existed more in words than in actions, a "phone father" whose love felt intangible, like a mirage she could never quite grasp.

As a child, Seven had clung to those promises, her heart swelling with hope each time the phone rang. She would picture him walking into her life, sitting in the front row at her school plays, clapping louder than anyone else. She imagined birthdays where he'd be there, lighting candles on her cake, his laughter filling the room. But those moments never came to life. Instead, her birthdays passed with cards that arrived late and presents picked out by someone else. The empty chair at her school events became a painful reminder of his absence.

Over time, her hope began to fracture, splintering under the weight of disappointment. Each broken promise widened the distance between them, stretching into a chasm too vast to cross. She dreaded his calls, not because she didn't want to hear his voice, but because every conversation was a painful reminder of what was absent. She'd pick up the phone, forcing herself to ignore the ache in her chest as he spoke of "next time," even though she already knew that "next time" was just another empty promise.

Derek's absence didn't just leave a void, it taught her how to live with disappointment. It taught her how to silence the ache in her chest, to swallow her hurt and pretend it didn't exist. She told herself it was enough and that the phone calls, the occasional gifts, the distant love were better than nothing. But deep down, she had always wanted more. She had wanted a father who showed up, who stayed, who didn't make her feel like she was always waiting for someone who would never come.

Now, as an adult, she could see the ripple effects of his absence everywhere. Derek had been the first man to teach her that love was conditional, fleeting, and unreliable. She saw shades of him in Rowan, who remained physically distant and emotionally unavailable, leaving her to shoulder the weight of their daughter Ryan's needs alone. She recognized his empty promises in Michael, whose smooth words and transient affections had only deepened her scars.

The realization hit her like a wave, she had spent her entire life waiting. Waiting for men to keep their promises, waiting for them to show up, waiting for them to prove they were different. But they never were. Every man who came into her life seemed to carry a piece of Derek with them, repeating the same patterns, leaving the same wounds. And with each disappointment, Seven's walls grew higher, her heart harder, her trust more fragile.

Her mind wandered back to those childhood nights when she lay in bed, staring at the ceiling, wondering what was so wrong with her that her father couldn't stay. She remembered how she would practice the words she wanted to say to him, how she would dream of telling him how much his absence hurt. But when the phone rang, all those words would evaporate. She didn't want to seem ungrateful or make him feel bad, so she buried her pain beneath a mask of indifference.

Now, as she stared out into the night, the ache in her chest felt both familiar and foreign. She had carried it for so long, it had become a part of her, shaping who she was. Derek had taught her many things, not by what he did, but by what he didn't do. He taught her that love could be withheld, that promises could be broken, and that she had to rely on herself because no one else was reliable.

But there was one thing he hadn't taken from her: her resolve. Though her trust was fragile and her heart guarded, she refused to let the cycle define her. Derek may have been a ghost in her life, but Seven was determined to be fully present for Ryan. She would not let her daughter feel the emptiness she had felt. The pain Derek left behind might have shaped her, but it would not control her.

And yet, in the quiet moments, when she allowed herself to feel the depth of her wounds, she couldn't help but wonder. Was she destined to carry this ache forever? Or was there still a way to let it go?

The Weight of Realization

The weight of everything crushed Seven like an invisible force, each memory and regret piling onto her chest until it felt impossible to breathe. Pain became her companion, raw, searing, and all-consuming. It wasn't just the betrayals, or the broken relationships; it was the realization that she had spent her entire life waiting for something—someone—to make her feel whole. And that wholeness had never come.

Seven sat at the foot of her bed, the quiet of the house amplifying the storm inside her. Shadows danced on the walls, mirroring the chaos within. She stared at the floor, her thoughts a swirling mix of anger, sorrow, and exhaustion. Trying to fix what was always broken: relationships with family, lovers, and even herself, had worn her down to the bone.

But amid the chaos, there was a flicker of something different: a yearning for freedom. The thought crept in slowly, quietly, but once it took hold, it wouldn't let go. What if she let it all go? What if she stopped trying to mend what was irreparable and instead escaped, to leave behind the weight of everyone else's expectations, betrayals, and demands?

Seven leaned back, staring at the ceiling. Walking away felt both selfish and terrifying, yet it also felt like a lifeline, a way to break free from the cycles that chained her. She didn't have to keep carrying the burden of her past. She could choose something different.

Her thoughts drifted to Ryan, her daughter's laughter ringing in her memory like a haunting melody. Ryan was her world, her light, her reason to keep going. But even that love came with its own weight. Seven wanted to be the mother Ryan could look up to, but lately, she felt like a failure. She had been distant, distracted, and consumed by her own pain. And the more she thought about it, the more she realized she was terrified of passing her own insecurities and fears onto her daughter.

"I don't want her to end up like me," Seven whispered into the empty room, her voice breaking.

As much as she loved Ryan, a part of her felt like she was drowning under the responsibility of being everything for someone else when she could barely hold herself together. The love she had for her daughter was boundless, but it didn't erase the cracks in her foundation. It didn't erase the resentment she felt toward the people who had failed her, the relationships that left her broken, or the isolation that had grown like a shadow in her life.

That night, as she tucked Ryan into bed, Seven felt the familiar pang of guilt. Ryan's tiny hand gripped hers, her love pure and unconditional, and for a moment, Seven's heart ached with the thought of leaving. She knelt beside her daughter, brushing a strand of hair from her forehead, and whispered, "I love you, baby girl."

Ryan's breathing slowed, her chest rising and falling in a peaceful rhythm that seemed to mock the chaos in Seven's soul.

The Push Toward Escape

The thought haunted her as she paced the house later that night, the silence pressing in from every corner. What if leaving wasn't abandonment but an act of survival? What if, by stepping away, she could finally find herself, rebuild the parts of her that had been chipped away by years of pain and disappointment?

Seven hated herself for even considering it, but the idea wouldn't let go. She couldn't shake the feeling that staying meant slowly unraveling, and if she unraveled, what would be left for Ryan?

She reflected on her relationships, the love she pursued, the validation she pleaded for, and the emptiness each relationship left her with. Michael's words still echoed in her mind, hollow and insincere: "I care about you, Seven. You know that, right?" And Rowan, with his fleeting presence and endless excuses, had left scars that would take years to heal. Even her mother, with her well-meaning but dismissive advice, had contributed to the deep-seated feeling that she was never enough.

Picking up her journal, Seven started to write, her emotions pouring onto the page. She wrote about her fears, her failures, and her longing for something more, something she couldn't quite define.

The Decision

By the time the first light of dawn stretched across the horizon, Seven had made up her mind. This wasn't a fleeting thought or a desperate plea for change, it was a resolution. She wasn't just leaving to escape; she was leaving to let go. The weight of staying had become unbearable, like a vice tightening around her soul, suffocating who she used to be.

Seven didn't plan to come back. The unknown ahead frightened her, but it also whispered promises of freedom and clarity, something she hadn't felt in years. Staying meant continuing to pour from an empty cup, pretending the cracks in her foundation didn't exist, hoping no one would notice the structure crumbling beneath her. She was done pretending.

As the morning light filtered through the blinds, painting the walls in soft hues, she looked around the house one final time. This wasn't just a place she was leaving; it was a life, a version of herself she could no longer be. Every corner carried a memory, but the memories were tangled with pain, unmet expectations, and a lingering sense of being trapped.

Seven's hands trembled as she packed her bag. Each item she placed inside felt like a piece of her old life being left behind. When she stepped into Ryan's room, her heart clenched so tightly it felt as if it might shatter. She stood over her daughter, watching her small chest rise and fall with each peaceful breath.

Leaning down, she kissed Ryan's forehead, her lips lingering for a moment, as if trying to imprint the memory. "I love you," she whispered, her voice barely audible, even to herself. Seven wasn't running from

Ryan; she was running for her. Because Seven knew that staying, broken and lost, would never allow her to be the mother Ryan deserved.

This wasn't an act of abandonment. It was a leap into the unknown, a desperate bid to rediscover the strength she once had and the woman she still hoped to become.

8

Shadows Beneath the Surface

Quietly, Seven moved around her bedroom, careful not to break the stillness of the morning. As she folded the last of Ryan's clothes and placed them gently into the dresser, a soft knock on the front door announced her mother's arrival. She took a steadying breath and went to open it, her mind already swirling with the unspoken weight of her plan for the day.

"Morning, sweetheart," Trisha greeted, her smile warm but tired, carrying the air of someone who'd made this early visit out of love and obligation alike. "How's my little angel doing?"

Seven forced a smile. "Still asleep. Thanks for coming so early, Mom. I just... I really need this break today."

Trisha stepped inside, a familiar mix of concern and practicality in her expression. She looked at Seven for a long moment, her eyes softening. "You've been pushing yourself too hard. I've seen it. Between work and trying to hold everything together, you're going to burn yourself out. You need to slow down."

"I'm fine, Mom," Seven replied, brushing the comment off, though her voice lacked conviction.

Trisha touched her arm gently. "I mean it, Seven. You've been doing so much since you got that promotion—too much. Don't feel bad about your success. You're building something, but you can't carry the world on your shoulders all at once."

Seven bit her lip, the tension in her chest tightening. "I'll try," she said, the words feeling hollow even as she spoke them.

Trisha gave her a knowing look, but didn't press further. She stepped toward Ryan's room, her voice lightening. "Go on, then. I've got things here. Take the time you need and don't feel guilty about it; we'll see you this evening."

Seven hesitated, glancing at the door to Ryan's room before nodding. "Thanks, Mom," she said softly. "I'll see you tonight."

The Journey Begins

As Seven drove, each mile stretched out the distance between her and the burdens she'd left behind. Her mother's words echoed faintly in her mind: You're building something... don't feel bad about your success. Trisha's support should have brought comfort, but instead, it deepened the ache in her chest. Seven had been running on fumes for so long, pushing herself to meet the expectations of everyone around her: her career, her family, her friends, even herself.

Now, the road ahead stretched endlessly, a literal and metaphorical path toward clarity, though the weight of her choices pressed heavily on her. Her thoughts churned like stormy seas, pulling her into the depths of her memories.

She thought about the weight of her family, friends, and all the complex ties that shaped her. These connections should have strengthened her, yet over the years, they had turned heavy and suffocating. Shadows lingered on each of them, darkening her memories with betrayal, envy, and a deep loneliness she'd never admitted out loud.

Her phone buzzed from the passenger seat. Michael. Her pulse hitched—out of habit, out of history—but the thrill was laced with something heavier. She already knew how this would go. The same cycle, the same empty pull. And yet, despite everything, his name still had the power to shake her.

"Not today," she muttered, gripping the steering wheel tighter. She ignored the call, letting it ring out, but the buzzing started again moments later.

The second call was harder to ignore. Seven pulled over to the side of the road and stared at the screen. For years, she allowed Michael to take up space in her mind, her heart, her life. Each call was a reminder of his hold on her, his ability to insert himself into her thoughts, even when she was trying to move forward.

She scrolled to his name, her finger hovering for only a moment before she blocked him. It wasn't just a gesture; it was a reckoning, a final unspoken vow to reclaim the pieces of herself he'd taken. She exhaled sharply, releasing the suffocating weight he placed on her for so long; and for the first time in years, she felt unshackled.

Shadows of Betrayal

As the miles ticked by, Seven allowed her mind to wander. The steady hum of the tires against the pavement provided a rhythm to the cascade of memories flooding her mind. Memories of Tanya and her sharp, cutting words resurfaced, slicing through her thoughts like jagged shards of glass. Tanya's resentment, born of jealousy, had always lingered beneath the surface, unspoken yet palpable, like a shadow in the corner of a room.

Seven thought of the Thanksgiving dinner where Tanya's disdain had spilled over, unfiltered and cruel. They had been seated at the crowded family table, laughter and conversation swirling around them like warm currents. Seven had been sharing a lighthearted story from high school, her cousins leaning in, laughing along, captivated by her natural charisma. Then, in a moment of silence that seemed almost timed, Tanya's voice had cut through the air.

"She just always has to be the center of attention, doesn't she?" Tanya muttered to another cousin, her tone laced with bitterness.

The sting of those words had stayed with Seven for years, echoing in her mind during quiet moments of self-reflection. She had never wanted to be the center of anything, never craved the spotlight in the way Tanya had implied. All she ever wanted was to be accepted for who she was, to feel a genuine connection with those around her, free of judgment or competition. But time and time again, her relationships—whether with family, friends, or lovers—had revealed cracks beneath the surface.

The betrayal wasn't always overt; sometimes it was subtle, like the coldness of a sidelong glance or the faint condescension in a tone of voice. Tanya had been one of the first to teach her that admiration could so easily turn into resentment.

Seven's thoughts drifted further, settling on her best friend from high school, Mia. They had been inseparable, sharing everything from their deepest fears to their wildest dreams. Mia had been Seven's confidante, someone she trusted implicitly. But even with Mia, the shadows of jealousy had crept in, poisoning the bond they had built over years.

Seven could still hear Mia's words, spoken during what would become their last argument. "It's always about you, Seven. You get everything without even trying."

The accusation had felt like a slap in the face. Seven had been blindsided, unable to process how the friend she had trusted most could harbor such resentment. Mia's insecurities, unknown to Seven, fueled her bitterness, a revelation as painful as the words themselves.

Those words, like Tanya's, had left a wound that never quite healed. Seven had spent so much of her life questioning herself, wondering if she was the problem, if she somehow invited the resentment and betrayal that seemed to follow her. She would comb through her actions, her words, her very essence, searching for the flaw that seemed to provoke such feelings in others.

Was it her confidence? Her beauty? Her achievements? Seven had never seen herself as someone to envy. If anything, she had times of battling her own insecurities. She had struggled to see the reflection others seemed to project onto her, a woman who "had it all."

Betrayal had become a refrain in her life, each verse sung by a different name—Tanya, Mia, Diane. Their jealousy, sometimes a quiet hum, sometimes a shattering crescendo, always ended the same way: abandonment. Each wound deepened her distrust, each disappointment another brick in the wall she built around herself. Now, she let no one too close—because history had taught her: that closeness always came at a cost.

She remembered one particular night in college when Mia's betrayal had come full circle. Seven had gone to a party, hopeful that she and Mia could repair their friendship. But as soon as she arrived, she saw Mia in the corner of the room, laughing with a group of people who had once been their mutual friends. They didn't acknowledge Seven's arrival, and Mia's eyes skimmed over her as if she were a stranger.

That hollow feeling in her chest had become familiar, as if each friend took a piece of her when they walked away, leaving her a little colder, a little less willing to trust. It wasn't just the loss of the friendship that hurt, it was the realization that the bond had never been as strong as she had believed.

Seven exhaled deeply, gripping the steering wheel tighter as the memories threatened to overwhelm her. The road stretched endlessly ahead, a blank canvas that she longed to fill with something new, something free from the shadows of her past. But the weight of those betrayals still clung to her like a heavy cloak, refusing to let go.

Her cousin Diane's words from years ago resurfaced, the warning laced with its own brand of bitterness: "You know, Seven, people don't always have your best interests at heart."

At the time, Seven had brushed it off, thinking Diane was simply feeding into family gossip. But as the years passed and her relationships continued to fracture, those words took on a deeper significance. Diane had been speaking from her own insecurities, projecting her fears and doubts onto Seven. Yet, there was a kernel of truth in her statement, one that Seven couldn't ignore. Trust, she had learned, was a fragile thing, easily broken and nearly impossible to repair.

The burden of other people's expectations and judgments weighed heavily on her. It was as though she had been carrying their insecurities along with her own, each one a tether that bound her to their approval. Each fractured friendship, each jealous glance, each family member's cold shoulder had taught her that trust was not only fragile but also fleeting.

As she reflected on these past relationships, she saw how they had stripped away her innocence, piece by piece. Each betrayal had left its mark, shaping her into the woman she was now: guarded, intuitive, and painfully attuned to the shadows in human nature. What was once a faint whisper of spiritual awareness had sharpened into an unrelenting force, honed by deception and doubt. Now, she could sense the hidden motives beneath carefully chosen words, the subtle shifts in energy that signaled envy or betrayal. It was both a gift and a curse—this ability to see people as they truly were.

Seven sighed, her breath fogging the air in front of her. She wanted to let go of the past, to shed the weight of betrayal and step into a future where trust and connection felt possible again. However, the scars ran deep, and the shadows of betrayal lingered, refusing to release their hold.

A World of Isolation

The road ahead felt infinite, a stark contrast to the confines of her past. Seven thought about her father, Derek, and the way his absence had shaped her understanding of love and loyalty. He had always been a voice on the phone, a distant presence who offered financial support but little else.

"Why couldn't he just show up?" Seven whispered to herself, the question hanging in the stillness of the car. Derek's absence had forced her to rely on herself, to fortify the walls that shielded her from the sting of those who couldn't, or wouldn't, stay.

But those walls had come at a cost. They had left her isolated, unable to fully trust even those who wanted to be there for her.

The Weight of Reflection

Seven's mind turned to her career, the one thing she had thrown herself into when everything else felt unstable. The promotion she had received months ago had been a milestone, but it came with its own pressures. She had been working longer hours, juggling more responsibilities, and feeling the growing weight of expectations from her colleagues and superiors. Success was just as heavy a burden as failure.

Her mother's words came back to her: You've been doing too much... don't feel guilty. But the guilt was inescapable. She couldn't shake the feeling that she was failing somewhere—at work, at home, or in her own heart.

Yet, as she drove further away from the city, a faint glimmer of something new began to emerge. Hope. Perhaps in the distance, away from the entanglements of her life, she could find the clarity she so desperately sought.

The Road Ahead

The road stretched endlessly before her, and for the first time in years, Seven felt the smallest flicker of freedom. It wasn't much—just a spark—but it was enough to keep her going. She rolled down the window slightly, letting the cool breeze rush in, its crispness biting her cheeks and carrying away the stale remnants of the life she was leaving behind. The hum of the engine and the rhythmic thrum of the tires on the asphalt created a soothing melody, a lullaby that quieted the chaos in her mind.

For the first time, the weight of others' expectations lifted, if only slightly. The shadows of betrayal, judgment, and resentment still lingered, clinging to the edges of her thoughts like stubborn cobwebs. But with every mile she put between herself and the life she was fleeing, they felt less oppressive, their hold on her loosening bit by bit. The city skyline that had once hemmed her in with its suffocating familiarity was now just a distant silhouette in her rearview mirror. Ahead, the open road beckoned, its vastness a promise of something new.

Seven whispered to herself, her voice steady but soft, "This is my chance. My chance to find myself again."

But even as the words escaped her lips, doubt crept in, curling around her resolve like tendrils of smoke. Could she really find herself out here, away from everything she'd ever known? Or was she simply running, hoping that distance alone could heal wounds too deep to ignore? She shook her head, gripping the steering wheel tighter. No. She wasn't running. Not this time. She was choosing herself—for the first time in far too long.

The road stretched endlessly before her, a blank slate waiting to be filled. Seven didn't know where she was going or what she would find, but for the first time, she was determined to discover it on her own terms. The uncertainty felt more like an invitation than a threat. Each mile was a declaration of her independence, a rejection of the chains that had held her captive for so long.

The past tugged at her, though, unwilling to let go without a fight. Her mind flickered with images of Ryan, her sweet daughter's face framed by wild curls, her laughter echoing in Seven's memory like a song she couldn't forget. Guilt gnawed at her, sharp and insistent. What kind of mother leaves her child behind? Seven's heart twisted painfully, the ache almost too much to bear.

Ahead, the horizon stretched endlessly, the pale light of dawn beginning to creep over the edges of the world. It illuminated the road in shades of gold and amber, transforming the path ahead into something almost sacred. Seven's resolve hardened. This was her journey, her time to reclaim the parts of herself she had lost in the world of betrayal, heartache, and unmet expectations.

The breeze through the open window carried a faint scent of pine and earth, grounding her in the present. She turned up the radio, letting the music fill the car, its rhythm syncing with the pounding of her heart. The lyrics spoke of freedom and self-discovery, a coincidence that felt like a sign. Seven allowed herself a small smile, the first genuine one in what felt like forever.

She wasn't sure what the future held. Maybe it would be messy, full of wrong turns and dead ends. But maybe it would be exactly what she needed. For now, the road was enough.

9

Whispers Along the Path

Seven's hands gripped the steering wheel with a mixture of fatigue and frustration, her mind still reeling from everything that led her here. The small, unmarked highway stretched out before her like a ribbon of nothingness, a desolate road with no real destination. She drove for hours, with nothing but the rhythmic hum of tires on asphalt to keep her company. The sky grew darker, the setting sun casting long shadows across the empty landscape. She was far from everything: far from the people she used to know, far from the tangled mess of her life. And yet, there was no peace to be found on the open road.

As she drove deeper into the unfamiliar stretch of road, a cold, unfamiliar sense of emptiness began to settle in her bones. The isolation was suffocating. Even though she escaped, there was still a part of her that felt trapped, like she was driving away from something she couldn't outrun. She hadn't quite figured out what that was, perhaps the heavy weight of her unresolved grief, or the overwhelming burden of all the broken relationships that never healed. But here, in the stillness, surrounded by nothing but miles of open road, she felt the weight of it more than ever.

Eventually, her eyes landed on a flickering neon sign up ahead: "Deer Creek Motel." The motel, old and worn, tucked away behind a thicket of trees that barely let any light through. The kind of place where travelers stopped when they had nowhere else to go. Seven turned in, the gravel crunching beneath the tires as she made her way toward the office. The building loomed in front of her like a forgotten relic, its paint chipped and faded. There was no warmth in the lights of the parking lot, no sense of comfort or safety. Just an old building in the middle of nowhere.

The front desk clerk, a man in his mid-forties with a thick, unshaven face, glanced up from his magazine as she entered. He didn't offer a smile, nor did he ask her anything beyond the standard check-in questions. Seven handed over the cash, and he handed her a key. There was no need for small talk, no interest in anything beyond the transaction. She was just another passerby in a place where time didn't matter, where people came and went without a trace.

When she reached the room, the door creaked as she opened it, revealing a small, dingy space with stained carpets and a musty smell that clung to the walls. The air was thick, heavy with an odor that made her want to gag. She stepped inside, kicking the door shut behind her. The bed was unmade; the sheets faded from years of use. The bathroom light buzzed incessantly, flickering in a manner that made her stomach tighten. But it was a place to rest. A temporary escape from the mess of her thoughts and emotions.

She dropped her bag onto the bed, its fabric scratching against the threadbare comforter. Her fingers trailed over the worn quilt, the rough texture of it reminding her of something distant and forgotten. She threw herself onto the bed, staring up at the cracked ceiling, her thoughts swirling in a chaotic dance.

She thought of her family, her cousins, especially. The ones who had been taken too soon. The ones she didn't have the chance to reconcile with before they were gone. The ones who died under tragic circumstances. She always thought she had more time, but time unfortunately run out before she had the chance to make amends. The guilt was suffocating. She couldn't stop thinking about the way their voices sounded the last time they spoke, the way they laughed when they were together. The way she had taken them for granted.

And then there was her mother. The one person she always hoped would understand, but who never did. Her every attempt to bridge the gap between them was met with cold distance. She tried to be the daughter her mother wanted, but it never seemed to be enough. Her mother had always moved on, and Seven had been left behind. In the quiet moments of her life, she yearned for the love and approval that would never come. She had shut herself off, learned to live in a world where her feelings were secondary to everyone else's.

Her mind drifted again, this time to Michael. He had been the constant in her life—when he wanted to be. The one person who had broken through her walls, only to leave her standing on the other side, wondering what went wrong. His promises had always been empty, his words like smoke—here one minute, gone the next. She wanted him to be the answer to all her questions. But he wasn't. He had never been. She had given so much of herself to him, to a relationship that had never been real. She had loved him, but it cost her more than she was willing to admit.

And Rowan, she thought of him, too. The man who had been a brief respite, a reminder that love and intimacy were still possible. But even he deceived her. Hiding his family, his life, from her. She had trusted him, but in the end, he only added to the list of broken promises. And now, she was left wondering if there was anyone who would ever show her the love and commitment she so desperately needed.

The room seemed to grow colder as the night stretched on; the temperature dropping just enough for her to notice. She pulled the thin, scratchy blanket over her shoulders, curling into herself, trying to ignore the creeping sense of discomfort. The silence, oppressive and thick with the weight of everything she had left behind. But it wasn't only the silence. There was something else, something unexplainable. The flickering of the bathroom light, the faint creaking of the floorboards. Every little sound seemed amplified in the stillness.

Seven sat up, the bed springs groaning beneath her. She glanced toward the bathroom, the door slightly ajar. There was something unsettling about it—something that made the hairs on the back of her neck stand up. She checked the room when she first entered, but now, alone in the dark, she wasn't so sure. She could have sworn she heard something, some sort of movement, a whisper in the silence. But when she looked again, there was nothing. Only the faint hum of the refrigerator, the faint rattle of the air conditioning unit.

She shook her head, trying to push the thoughts away. It was just the isolation and the darkness creeping in. She hadn't been alone in a while, and it began playing tricks on her mind. But no matter how much she tried to convince herself otherwise, the unease lingered.

The sound of a distant car passing broke the silence, its headlights briefly cutting through the oppressive darkness outside. Seven glanced up, her attention drawn to the way the beams danced across the parking lot, casting long, warped shadows over the cracked concrete. But something about the car's movement made her uneasy. It didn't feel like a normal passing vehicle. The lights moved slower than they should have, lingering just long enough to make her stomach tighten.

It felt as though the driver was lingering just out of sight: observing, waiting for something, or perhaps someone. Seven's breath hitched, her heartbeat thundering in her ears. She edged closer to the window, staying just behind the thin curtain, and dared a glance outside. The car drove away, its engine's low growl retreating into the distance, yet the unsettling feeling of being watched clung to her like a shadow.

Her gaze lingered on the empty parking lot, her eyes scanning every corner for signs of movement. The barren stretch of gravel and broken asphalt offered no comfort, just an unyielding sense of isolation. She stepped back from the window, the thin fabric fluttering back into place, but the unease clung to her like a second skin.

She paced the small room, her bare feet sinking into the frayed, faded carpet, each step leaving an imprint.

Shadows lurked in every corner, darkness pooling in crevices that hinted at unseen threats. But the unease ran deeper than the room itself; it clung to the unnatural stillness, a quiet that pulsed with unspoken tension. This silence held no peace. It hung heavy, charged, like the air before a thunderstorm, thick with something unseen, waiting to break.

Seven rubbed her arms, trying to smooth the goosebumps prickling her skin. The walls pressed closer, the space tightening with each passing second. The air was heavier now, harder to breathe, as though the room itself conspired against her.

"Get it together," she whispered to herself, her voice trembling.

But her body wouldn't listen. Her chest tightened, her breath quickening into shallow gasps. She pressed a hand to her sternum, willing her racing heart to calm, but the harder she tried, the worse it became. She felt trapped, caged by her own mind.

And then she heard it.

A faint sound drifted through the room, like whispers riding the wind. Her head snapped up, eyes scanning the dim space. Not loud, just a soft, elusive murmur brushing the edges of her awareness. She forced herself to believe it was nothing, a trick of the mind. But the whispers lingered, teasing, taunting, slipping through her consciousness like a cold draft seeping through a crack in the wall.

Her gaze landed on the bathroom door, slightly ajar. The flickering light inside cast erratic shadows across the tiles, making the space seem alive in a way that made her stomach churn. She moved toward it slowly; her steps hesitant, her breath caught in her throat.

The cracked mirror above the sink reflected her image back at her, but it wasn't the Seven she recognized. The woman staring back looked haunted: her eyes red and hollow, her face ashen and drawn. She looked like a stranger, someone worn down by years of fear and regret.

Her trembling fingers gripped the edge of the sink as she stared into her reflection, searching for a trace of the person she used to be. "This isn't real," she whispered, her voice barely audible over the buzz of the light above her. "You're just tired. You're imagining things."

But the whispers grew louder.

Seven spun around, her heart hammering in her chest. The room stood empty, yet something pressed in around her—an unseen presence, thick and suffocating. The shadows deepened, stretching, as if inching closer with each passing second.

Then a faint *click* echoed from the wall.

Seven's eyes darted toward the source. On a shelf, a small, weathered clock sat, its delicate mechanism jerking into motion. The door above it snapped open, revealing a nightingale bird; its feathers dull, chipped, and worn with age. Instead of the vibrant song that should have poured forth, the bird gave a meek, rasping chirp, so faint and frail it seemed to gasp for life. The sound sliced through the heavy silence, too soft yet strangely piercing, like something once full of beauty now strangled by time. The bird's wings fluttered stiffly, unnaturally, as if it had forgotten how to move with grace. A reluctant clanking echoed as the bird retreated, disappearing back into the clock with a hollow *thunk,* leaving the room colder and quieter than before. The nightingale, once the voice of beauty, was now only a sad, broken echo.

The room fell silent once more, but it wasn't the same. The air had thickened.

A sudden knock at the door shattered the stillness.

Seven jumped, the sharp sound sending a jolt of adrenaline through her veins. Her breath caught, her eyes snapping toward the door. The knock came again, soft and hesitant, but insistent enough to make her skin crawl.

"Who's there?" she called, her voice steadier than she felt.

No response.

Another knock—louder, more urgent. Seven's hand hovered over the doorknob, her fingers trembling. She didn't know why, but every instinct screamed at her not to open it. Her chest tightened as she stood there, frozen in place, the seconds stretching into an eternity.

The knocking stopped.

Seven pressed her ear to the door, straining to hear any sound from the other side. The silence was deafening, broken only by the faint *drone* of the refrigerator and the erratic buzzing of the bathroom light.

Finally, she reached for the lock, her fingers trembling as she slid the chain free. Her hand paused on the knob, a cold sweat breaking out along her skin. She didn't want to open it, but the not knowing was worse. With a deep breath, she turned the handle and pulled the door open.

The parking lot was empty.

No one stood on the other side. No footsteps echoed in the stillness. Just the same oppressive quiet that had plagued her since she arrived.

Seven shut the door quickly, locking it and sliding the chain back into place. Her hands trembled as she leaned against the door, her breath coming in shallow gasps. The whispers were gone now, but the unease remained, curling around her like a vice.

She sank onto the edge of the bed, her knees drawn to her chest, her arms wrapped tightly around them. The room felt colder, the shadows darker, as though the motel itself was alive and watching her. She tried to tell herself it was just her imagination, just her mind playing tricks on her after everything she'd been through. But deep down, she wasn't sure.

The feeling of being watched wouldn't go away.

10

Confronting the Abyss

S even stared at her phone, the bright red battery icon flashing ominously at her: 7%. The tightness in her chest escalated with every passing second as her heart raced. She cursed under her breath, gripping the phone like a lifeline, knowing how vulnerable she was about to become. Alone. In a strange place. Completely disconnected. The isolation felt palpable, settling in like a suffocating fog. The thought of her phone dying—of being severed from the world—made her stomach twist into knots.

"Shit," she muttered, slipping the phone into her pocket. The weight of it, the quiet stillness around her, felt so oppressive. The room was too small, too confining. And the buzz from the neon sign outside, faint but incessant, gnawed at her nerves like an irritating itch she couldn't scratch. She needed to leave. She needed to get that charger and come back, but something was wrong.

Just get the charger. Then, come back.

The thought did nothing to ease her anxiety. The air inside the room felt thick, pressing in on her from every direction. There was no escape from it. She quickly grabbed her room key from the nightstand and shoved it into her pocket. The door felt like a threshold between her sanity and something darker. She had to push through.

She put on her sneakers, but before stepping out, she hesitated. Her hand hovered on the doorknob. She stood there for what felt like an eternity, her breath shallow as she listened. The air outside was too still, and the silence seemed to carry a burden, as though the world had paused to watch her. There was something in that stillness that felt wrong. Almost predatory. Her instincts, usually sharp, were screaming at her to stay inside. But she had no choice.

Taking a steadying breath, she cracked the door open. The night air hit like a cold slap, sharp and biting. Darkness yawned before her, vast and impenetrable. Above, the neon sign sputtered in uneven bursts, its sickly glow casting warped shadows that twitched and stretched like living things. The pavement lay fractured and worn, and as she stepped forward, the gravel grated beneath her sneakers, echoing too loudly, as if the ground itself was holding its breath.

She walked quickly, her eyes darting around, every little noise amplified in the vast emptiness around her. The flicker of the neon light above cast eerie, elongated shadows across the parking lot, and her every step felt too loud, too obvious. She could feel the eyes of the night on her, the air heavy with a sense of being watched. Every instinct screamed at her to turn back, but she couldn't. The thought of her phone dying and being alone in that room, in this desolate place—was worse.

Halfway to her car, she saw him. The motel clerk.

He was standing near the office, leaning against the doorframe, a cigarette dangling from his lips. The faint glow of the ember illuminated his greasy face in brief flashes. His clothes hung loosely around his body, stained and unkempt. His massive, unshaven belly protruded from underneath a poorly fitted shirt, and his fingers were thick, stained yellow at the tips from years of smoking. His grin, stretched across his face like a grotesque mask, was uneven, some teeth missing, others jagged and yellowed.

He didn't move as Seven approached, his gaze following her every step, lingering far too long.

"Need somethin', darlin'?" he drawled, the words thick with a slow, southern drawl. The tone was thick with something else too, a hint of something predatory, and Seven felt it immediately. An icy shiver ran down her spine.

Seven's heart raced. She stopped in her tracks, forcing herself to stand tall. Her voice came out steady, though it was hard to disguise the slight tremor that vibrated through her words. "Just grabbing my charger," she said, her voice more clipped than she intended. She forced a polite smile, but her fists clenched at her sides, tension coiling like a spring within her.

The clerk didn't answer, but his eyes flicked over her body with a deliberate slowness that made her skin crawl. He took another drag from his cigarette; the ember flaring bright and momentarily lighting up his face like some kind of grotesque, shadowy figure.

"Well, ain't you brave, wanderin' out here all by yourself?" he murmured, the laughter that followed rumbling low in his chest. "You are out here by yourself, right?" The sound was unsettling, like an old truck rattling down a long-abandoned road.

Seven didn't answer. She turned on her heel and picked up her pace, but his eyes burned into her back, following her every move. The heaviness of his gaze stayed with her, gnawing at her insides. She quickened her steps, the crunch of gravel louder than it should have been, and finally reached her car.

Her fingers trembled as she unlocked the door. She snatched up the charger from the passenger seat, shooting a glance over her shoulder to see if the clerk had moved. He was still standing by the office, but the way he was watching her now sent a sickening feeling crawling up her spine.

Seven shoved the charger into her pocket and turned to head back to the room. She didn't even make it halfway before she froze.

A figure loomed in the far corner of the parking lot, half-devoured by shadows. Seven's breath hitched, her pulse slamming against her ribs.

It was him, the man from earlier, standing just as still, just as silent. Even in the dim light, his presence was suffocating. The wide-brimmed hat draped his face in shadow, but as he shifted, a sliver of his features caught the sickly neon glow. One of his eyes was sealed shut, fused unnaturally, as if the skin had been melted together. No patch. No scar. Just an absence where something vital should be.

The breath stalled in her throat. Something shifted at his side.

A massive Rottweiler sat beside him, its broad, muscular frame coiled with tension. The dog's chest rose and fell in slow, measured breaths, but its unblinking gaze, fixed on her, sent a cold ripple through her limbs. Her stomach twisted as the neon light flickered, casting strange shadows across its face.

One of its eyes sealed shut. Just like its owner.

Seven's fingers curled into fists. A sick sort of symmetry hung between them—man and beast, both marked by the same eerie affliction, both watching her with a strange stillness.

A low, guttural growl rumbled from the dog's throat, vibrating through the pavement beneath her feet.

The breath she had been holding slipped out in a shallow exhale.

The snarl deepened.

Then, with terrifying force, the dog lunged.

A savage bark ripped through the air as the leash yanked taut. Its claws scraped against the pavement, teeth flashing in the night light.

Seven flinched, the sound splitting through her bones like a whip crack.

The man never reacted.

His grip on the leash remained steady, fingers wrapped tight, motionless. His nails, long and thick with grim, curled slightly as if clutching something unseen. He didn't speak. Didn't move. Just stood there, watching her with that single, knowing eye.

Then, finally, in a voice too calm, and too smooth, he murmured, "Good boy."

The dog growled, still thrashing against the leash, but the man remained eerily composed, his face unreadable beneath the brim of his hat.

Seven took a step back. Then another. The moment she turned, she quickened her pace. She reached for the door, her hands shaking as she shoved the key into the lock, fumbling with it before it finally turned, and quickly slamming the door shut behind her, locking and bolting it then sliding the chain into place.

She ran a hand through her hair, breath uneven.

"What in the actual fuck was that?"

Seven leaned against the door, her chest heaving as she tried to steady her breath. The room was smothering with silence, pressing down on her. She plugged her charger into the nightstand outlet and waited. Nothing. The phone stayed dim and charge unresponsive. Her brow furrowed, panic creeping up her spine.

The electricity was out.

Every outlet in the room, every flick of the light switch, resulted in nothing. The room was chilly, and her phone's screen flashed briefly before it showed 6% battery.

Seven's breath caught in her throat. The feeling of being close to disconnection—trapped in this strange, hostile place—was suffocating. She paced the room, her thoughts spiraling faster than she could control.

A soft knock at the door made her freeze. Her breath caught in her chest, her heart hammering so loudly she thought it would burst from her ribs.

The knock came again, soft but insistent. Her pulse quickened. She glanced around, looking for a way out, a way to protect herself from whatever was happening, whatever this was.

Another knock—louder now.

Seven moved cautiously toward the door, her breath shallow as she pressed her ear against it. Her hand hovered above the doorknob, but she didn't turn it. She couldn't. She didn't know who it was, what they wanted, and she couldn't trust herself to make the right decision.

She backed away from the door slowly, the room closing in on her. Her body trembled, her knees weak. The world outside this room—if there was a world left—was closing in. And whatever was waiting out there wasn't human. It wasn't real.

She sat on the bed, clutching her phone, staring at the screen, hoping for even a wi-Fi signal. The scratching started again: soft at first, deliberate, like fingernails dragging across the glass.

Seven's stomach twisted. She couldn't stay here. But the door was locked. The windows were shut tight. The sounds, the presence—whatever was happening—was closing in on her, and she could do nothing to stop it.

11

The Weight of Wishes

S even lay on the lumpy, discolored mattress of the motel bed, the stench of stale cigarettes and mildew melting into the air, pressing in on her with no escape. The erratic flicker of the ceiling light buzzed, its unstable glow amplifying the tension in the already heavy air. The blanket she pulled around her shoulders was thin, rough against her skin, but it was the best she could do in a place like this. Her body was exhausted, but her mind raced with chaos, thoughts of the long, endless hours she'd driven, the overwhelming solitude that now defined her life, and the unsettling encounter with the motel clerk. Every detail of that moment, the way his eyes lingered on her, the way the shadows outside had seemed to stretch unnaturally, gnawed at her like an unhealed wound.

She closed her eyes tightly, trying to drown out the constant hum of her surroundings. It was hard to focus, but she knew she needed to escape the terror in her mind, even if just for a moment. She needed to shut it all out. Slowly, her body relaxed, the tension in her chest loosening just a little as the weariness settled in.

Then her mind took her somewhere else.

The dream came slowly, softly, like the gentle pull of a tide. At first, it was difficult to sink into it. The eerie atmosphere of the motel clung to her thoughts, but gradually, she drifted away from it, slipping into something softer, something more familiar. She could feel the warmth of the sun on her skin, the soft breeze brushing through the air, and she was no longer alone. She was in a beautiful garden, the kind she had always imagined in her more peaceful moments. It was filled with vibrant flowers, their colors rich and alive. The air was sweet with the scent of blooming roses and jasmine, each breath filling her with a sense of comfort she hadn't known in years.

Laughter echoed in the distance, a sound so pure, so joyful that it made Seven smile without thinking. She looked down at herself and saw that she was wearing a stunning white gown—its intricate lace detailing was like something out of a fairy tale, hugging her in all the right places, flowing out in a long, delicate train that shimmered with each subtle movement. Her hair cascaded in soft curls around her face, and she was holding a bouquet of fresh flowers in her hands—pale pink peonies and white lilies, their fragrance overwhelming in the most pleasant way.

Seven turned, and there, at the end of the aisle, was Michael. He stood tall in a perfectly tailored tuxedo, his tie matching the soft pastel shades of the flowers she held. His smile, radiant and filled with warmth, made her heart flutter. His eyes never left hers—there was a depth of emotion in them, a promise of something unbreakable. Seven took a step forward, her feet feeling light, as if she were walking on air. The grass beneath her felt soft and cool, each step like a note in a symphony she hadn't realized she'd been waiting to hear.

The surrounding guests were familiar faces: her family, her friends, everyone she loved and cherished. There, in the front row, her mother was beaming with pride. For the first time, she looked at Seven with a sense of warmth and understanding; her gaze was softer than Seven had ever seen it. Next to her sat her father, his arm around her mother, and for once, there was no tension, no bitterness between them. They were together, at peace. Seven's heart swelled at the sight of them. Her siblings sat beside her, smiling, their bond stronger than ever.

And then there was Ryan, her beautiful daughter, standing at the front with her flower girl dress, twirling and laughing with the innocence of youth. Seven couldn't help but smile as Ryan's curls bounced with each spin, her tiny hands scattering rose petals in her wake. It felt like the world had finally aligned—everything she had ever dreamed of was here, right in front of her.

As the ceremony progressed, Seven felt a deep sense of belonging, of completeness. Michael's vows were full of love, devotion, and promises of forever. The promises that made her believe in them, in their future. Seven could feel the strength of his words, but more importantly, she felt the depth of his love. She spoke her vows with a voice that rang clear and strong, filled with certainty.

"I'll love you forever," she said. "Through everything. You're my home."

The ceremony transitioned smoothly into the celebration. There was laughter, clinking glasses, and the hum of a perfect night. Seven looked around at the people who had been a part of her journey, and for the first time they were all smiling, dancing, enjoying the moment. Even her mother and father were on the dance floor, their movements graceful and in sync. For the first time in years, they weren't the parents who fought; they were the parents who celebrated, who supported their daughter.

Seven's heart overflowed as she watched Ryan play with her cousins, her laughter bright and contagious, filling the room with a lightness that made everything feel right. Michael was holding their baby, lifting the child into the air, and Seven could hear the child's delighted giggles, ringing like music. It was everything she had ever wanted.

Time shifted seamlessly, and now Seven found herself in a home, one far beyond what she had ever imagined. It was cozy yet elegant, filled with light and warmth. Every corner felt like it belonged to her, like she had created it herself. Michael was by her side as they prepared dinner together. The aroma of fresh herbs and spices filled the air, making Seven's stomach growl in anticipation. Ryan sat at the counter, coloring, while the baby napped nearby in a bassinet.

"Dinner smells amazing," Michael said, pressing a kiss to her cheek, his voice thick with appreciation.

Seven smiled, her heart full. She was happy. Her life was full of everything she needed. She wasn't empty anymore.

In the evenings, Michael and Seven sat on the porch, hand in hand, watching as Ryan ran through the yard, chasing fireflies in the summer air. The baby cooed happily in her lap, and Michael kissed her temple, whispering into her hair, "This is everything I've ever dreamed of."

Their love was simple, peaceful, and strong. They supported each other, worked together, and their home was a sanctuary. They worked together, raising their children with love, stability, and care. There were no shadows hanging over their heads.

Her career flourished, too. Seven had found her purpose in running a successful business, one that filled her with pride. She was respected by her peers and admired in her community. She felt fulfilled in every way possible.

The dream shifted again, and Seven found herself surrounded by her entire family during a holiday celebration. The warmth of the house, the laughter, the love—they were all here. Her parents, side by side, her siblings gathered around the table, her children playing together in the background, and Michael beside her, holding their youngest child.

Ryan rushed to her, her face glowing with excitement, a handmade ornament clutched in her tiny hands. "Look, Mommy! I made this for our tree!"

Seven knelt down, her heart full, and pulled Ryan into a tight embrace. "It's perfect," she whispered, tears spilling from her eyes as she kissed her daughter's forehead.

Her life, her whole life, this was everything she had always dreamed of. A loving family, a fulfilling career, peace. The burdens of the past had melted away. Her dreams were no longer just fantasies—they were real. They were here. This was happiness.

But then, as the music played on, the laughter faded. The colors in her dream began to fade too—like the vibrant hues of the world were being drained away, replaced by a dull, gray fog. The warmth she had felt slipped, fading into coldness. Seven's hand reached out toward Michael's, but he was far away now. His face, once filled with love, now looked distant. The vibrant world around her shrank until it was just a blur of shapes and figures.

The dream, which had been so real, so vivid, evaporated before her eyes. Seven's eyes fluttered open, her body jerking awake.

The faint light of the motel room buzzed above her, its low hum snapping her back to reality. The stale air of the room filled her lungs. The smell of mildew was thick in the air, the faded, stained ceiling just above her head. Her heart ached as the remnants of the dream drifted from her mind, fading into nothingness.

Tears welled in her eyes, and she rolled onto her side, curling up on the uncomfortable bed, a soft sob escaping her lips. The world she had dreamed of was slipping through her fingers, an illusion she could never grasp. The reality of her present, in this room, this life—was all she had now. The dream had been a glimpse, a taste of what could have been, but it was gone now. And she was left with the weight of it, heavy in her chest.

Seven clutched the scratchy blanket tighter around her, trying to pull warmth from it, but it felt as if the coldness was already inside her, clawing at her from the inside out. The dream was all she had left to hold on to, but it was just that—a dream.

12

A New Path

Seven stood by the cracked window, her eyes fixed on the barren parking lot. The silence in the motel room was suffocating, the quiet that wasn't truly still but instead seemed alive, humming with an undercurrent of something unseen. The flickering neon sign outside pulsed faintly through the window, casting uneven shadows across the stained carpet.

Her eyes drifted to the cheap plastic clock mounted on the wall, its hands at 3:33. It didn't tick, didn't move, just hung there in useless defiance of time. Seven furrowed her brow, the sight unnerving her more than she cared to admit.

"Guess time doesn't matter in this place anyway," she muttered under her breath, letting out a sigh as she tore her gaze away.

The room seemed to press in on her, its stale air thick with the smell of mildew, cheap cleaning products, and something else—something faintly metallic, like rust. Her fingers curled into the fabric of her jeans, gripping tightly as if anchoring herself to the present might stop her spiraling thoughts.

It wasn't working. The stillness only amplified the chaos in her mind. The faces of the motel clerk, the man in black, and the weight of her decisions all blurred together into a cacophony of unease. She felt watched even here, alone, as if the walls themselves had eyes.

Seven turned back to the parking lot. The man in black was still there, a shadowed figure leaning against the far wall of the motel. His silhouette was sharp against the dim light, and though she couldn't see his face, she could feel his presence like a tangible weight. He hadn't moved, hadn't even shifted his stance since she first noticed him hours ago.

Her chest tightened. She needed to leave.

A Stop at Rusty's

Inside, the air was thick, musty, and laced with an indefinable sourness. The shelves were sparsely stocked with outdated snacks and faded cans, all cloaked in a thin layer of dust. A rack of long-expired candy bars sagged in the corner, the wrappers faded and brittle.

Behind the counter stood a woman.

Seven took her in with a glance and immediately felt a shiver crawl up her spine. The clerk's brownish-blondish hair hung limp and greasy, sticking to her face in stringy clumps. Her mismatched eyes were impossible to ignore—one a piercing green, sharp and uncomfortably focused, the other a cloudy, milky grey that drooped halfway shut as though it couldn't bear to stay open.

The clerk leaned against the counter with an air of disinterest, her thin frame partially hidden behind a stained apron. There was a heaviness to her presence, as if she'd been sitting there for years, absorbing the gloom of the station like a sponge.

Seven grabbed a bottle of water from the cooler, the plastic cool and faintly sticky under her fingers. She wiped her hand on her jeans before approaching the counter, each step careful, the silence amplifying every sound she made.

The clerk didn't glance up right away. Her bony fingers traced the frayed edges of a yellowed, torn newspaper spread across the counter. When she finally lifted her gaze, it was sharp and uneven, locking with Seven's.

"Long night?" the clerk asked, her voice gravelly and slow, as though she rarely had cause to use it.

Seven forced a polite nod, her discomfort palpable. "Yeah, you could say that."

The clerk scanned the water bottle with deliberate slowness, her movements exaggerated and almost theatrical. Seven clenched her jaw, fighting the urge to snap at her to hurry.

"Be careful out there," the clerk said suddenly, her tone flat yet laced with something strange—something unsettling.

Seven's eyes narrowed. "Why?"

The clerk tilted her head slightly, her milky grey eye twitching as though it were attempting to focus. "Strange things happen on these roads."

Seven felt a sharp sting of irritation. Her patience, already worn thin from the day, was quickly unraveling. "What kind of strange things?" she asked, leaning forward slightly. "Do you care to elaborate, or do you just like saying creepy shit for the fun of it?"

The clerk's lips curled into a crooked smirk, revealing jagged, yellowed teeth. Her laugh came out as a harsh, grating chuckle, more like the sound of something breaking than genuine humor. "You'd think you'd want less to think about tonight," she said cryptically.

Seven's frustration boiled over. She snatched the bottle from the counter and slammed a crumpled bill down with more force than necessary. "Keep the change," she muttered, her tone sharp and cold.

As she turned to leave, the bell above the door jangled faintly, the sound grating against her nerves. She stepped into the chilly night air, taking a deep breath to calm herself. The tension in her chest refused to dissipate.

Glancing back, she saw the clerk emerge from behind the counter.

Seven froze for a moment, her eyes locking onto the woman as she moved awkwardly into view. It was then she noticed the clerk's wooden leg. The prosthetic was rough and unfinished; the wood splintered in places and mismatched against her other leg's pale, thin frame. The clerk's uneven gait sent a chill down Seven's spine as she limped toward the glass door.

The clerk stopped just inside; her mismatched eyes fixed on Seven's car with a disrupting intensity. Her crooked smirk remained, her head tilting slightly as though she were studying Seven, trying to peer into her very soul.

Seven's breath hitched as she climbed into her car and locked the doors. She turned the key, the engine roaring to life, and her hands tightened on the steering wheel.

As she pulled out of the lot, her eyes peeled on the rearview mirror. The clerk had stepped outside now, leaning against the doorframe with her wooden leg bent awkwardly. Her gaze followed the car as it disappeared into the night.

Seven's chest felt tight, her heartbeat erratic. Even when the gas station was far behind her, the image of that crooked smirk and those piercing mismatched eyes stayed with her, haunting the edges of her thoughts.

A Growing Unease

The darkness outside felt thicker now, heavier, as if the gas station itself had drained the air of its vitality. Seven climbed back into her car after a quick rest stop, locking the doors out of instinct. The faint glow of the gas station's lights cast long, distorted shadows across the lot, but everything seemed still.

Too still.

As she reached for the ignition, her eyes caught movement in the rearview mirror. Her breath hitched as she turned, squinting into the shadows.

There it was, a figure, partially obscured by the rusted truck at the edge of the lot. The hair on the back of her neck stood on end as she stared, her pulse quickening.

The figure shifted slightly, just enough for her to make out the outline of a man. His posture was eerily similar to that of the man in black back at the motel: silent, still, and unnervingly watchful.

Her fingers fumbled over the keys as she started the car, the engine roaring to life and breaking the oppressive silence. She gripped the wheel tightly, her eyes darting between the mirror and the figure.

As she pulled out of the rest stop, her headlights illuminated the area briefly. The figure was gone.

The Clock That Wouldn't Change

The highway stretched ahead, dark and endless. Seven's hands gripped the wheel tightly, her knuckles white against the leather. The events at the gas station churned in her mind, the clerk's cryptic words echoing like a warning she couldn't ignore.

She glanced at the dashboard clock. 3:36 a.m.

Her stomach twisted. She hadn't been driving for long, but she was sure more time had passed than that. She shook her head, dismissing the unease creeping into her thoughts. It was just a glitch, nothing more.

But the clock on the dashboard mirrored the one back at the motel. At the same time. The same unyielding stillness.

A faint buzz filled the car, the radio switching on by itself. Static poured through the speakers, loud and jarring. Seven's hands flew to the dials, twisting them in a frantic attempt to turn it off. The static grew louder, more insistent, until it cut off abruptly, leaving only silence.

Her heart pounded in the absence of sound. She stared at the dashboard again. 3:33 a.m.

"What the hell?" she whispered, her voice trembling.

The road ahead seemed to stretch infinitely, the darkness deepening with every mile. It felt less like she was escaping and more like she was being pulled toward something, something she couldn't see but could feel—a weight pressing against her chest, a whisper brushing against her ears.

Her eyes darted to the side mirror. For a brief moment, she thought she saw the figure again, a shadow standing still at the edge of the road. She blinked, and it was gone.

Seven's grip on the wheel tightened as she pressed harder on the accelerator, the engine roaring in protest. She couldn't shake the feeling that she wasn't alone, that the gas station, the motel, the frozen clocks; all of it was connected in some way she didn't yet understand.

The clock on the dashboard flickered suddenly, the numbers distorting before settling back to 3:33 a.m.

Her voice cracked as she whispered, "This can't be real."

But the road stretched on, dark and unyielding, and she wasn't sure what was real anymore.

13

Embracing the Journey

As the days stretched into weeks, the weight of Seven's decision began to lift, ever so slowly, as if the world itself were offering her a gentle reprieve. The relentless noise of her past had quieted in the wilderness, replaced by a symphony of rustling leaves, distant bird calls, and the soft murmur of a stream nearby. The forest was her new home, and for the first time in a long while, she felt the sweetness of solitude.

The woods had a magic all their own, casting a veil of peace over her that was both unfamiliar and comforting. She had learned how to build a fire, how to forage for berries, how to sleep under the stars without fear. There was an overwhelming sense of freedom here, a place where no one knew her, no one expected anything from her, and for the first time in what felt like forever, she wasn't worried about disappointing anyone. There were no angry words, no grudges, no fake smiles to navigate. There was only the earth beneath her, the sky above, and the quiet hum of her own heartbeat.

Seven had fallen into a rhythm, a strange sort of harmony with her new life. Each day felt like an adventure, full of small victories. She woke with the sun, stretched her limbs toward the sky, and smiled as the day greeted her like an old friend. The wind seemed to whisper through the trees, carrying away the ghosts of her past, replacing them with the sweet scent of pine and fresh earth.

The smell of wood smoke at dusk, the gleam of light in the trees as the evening settled, and the crunch of dry leaves beneath her boots—all of it felt so natural, so right. She didn't think about her dead phone and stopped worrying about the clock. Time had become something that happened in the background, irrelevant to the steady beat of the surrounding forest. She focused on the present, and it was enough.

Seven wasn't sure when she started to feel at home here, but it came on so gradually that it was almost imperceptible. The small acts of survival became less of a burden and more of a meditation. She found that working with her hands, collecting firewood, preparing a meal from foraged roots, and even setting up camp for the night brought a quiet satisfaction. She felt herself growing stronger with each passing day, but it wasn't just physical strength that she was gaining. It was a deep, emotional resilience, a sense of knowing that no matter what happened, she could make it through.

There were moments when she felt entirely alone in the world, and yet she didn't mind. For once, she didn't crave company or validation. The silence became a friend. It was the first time in years that she hadn't felt the pressure of needing to explain herself, needing to prove her worth. There was no need to answer anyone's questions, no expectations from friends or family. It was just her and the wilderness.

"Maybe I made the right choice," she thought one afternoon as she sat on a large rock by the stream, watching the water flow endlessly over smooth stones. She could see the reflection of the sun dancing on the surface, and for a moment, the world seemed perfect. Her mind drifted to thoughts of Ryan, the little girl she missed more than words could express. She thought of her smile, her laugh, the way her tiny hands would hold on to her when they crossed the street. Ryan's absence was a dull ache in her chest, but she held onto the belief that her daughter was safe, loved, and surrounded by the people who cared for her.

The ache was always there, especially at night when the firelight flickered in the darkness, and she could hear the distant hoot of an owl or the rustle of leaves in the breeze. It reminded her of the quiet nights when she would lie in bed, her daughter curled up beside her, listening to her breath in the dark. But she knew this decision was for the best. Ryan would be okay.

But for now, it was just Seven and the wilderness. And in this moment, it was enough.

The trees became her teachers, the wind her confidante. She'd grown accustomed to the calls of the birds, the way the morning mist hung heavy in the branches before it dissolved into sunlight. She learned which plants were safe to eat and which ones were best avoided. The world was simpler here, clearer. There was no room for complexity in her new life.

Sometimes, in the stillness of the evening, she would sit by the fire and reflect. She had become an expert at listening—listening to the world around her, but more importantly, listening to herself. In the quiet, her thoughts had become more focused. The anger she once carried seemed to ebb away, replaced by a clarity that had been missing for so long.

"Maybe I really did need this," she whispered to herself as the wind rustled through the trees. "Maybe this was the only way I could breathe again."

The tranquility of her surroundings made her feel untouchable, like she was living in a world where only good things could happen. Every evening, as the sun dipped below the horizon and painted the sky in shades of purple and gold, she would sit by the fire, her thoughts drifting toward the future. It seemed so simple, so clear. She had chosen this life, and it was hers to shape. It was her decision to make.

But despite the serenity, there was a growing tension in the back of her mind, a whispering thought that refused to be silenced. Michael.

She could feel his presence in the shadows of her mind, a reminder of what she'd left behind. No matter how much she tried to push it away, the anger would resurface. She wasn't done with him yet, not in her heart.

"He deserves to feel my pain," she muttered, more to herself than anyone else, the bitterness rising up again. A surge of satisfaction flowed through her as she imagined confronting him, making him see the damage he had caused. "He deserves to see what he did to me." "I'm done chasing things that will never be," she thought one night as she lay in her shelter, the stars above her twinkling like tiny diamonds scattered across a velvet sky. "I don't need him to apologize. I don't need him to understand. I need to understand myself."

Her hands clenched into fists as she stared into the fire, the flames dancing wildly in the night. The fantasy of it all was intoxicating, even though she knew deep down that it would never happen. That confrontation—where she would make him understand — was just a fleeting illusion. She had never been good at confronting the people who hurt her. It had always been easier to run, easier to escape.

But in her dreams, she was strong. She saw herself standing face-to-face with him, telling him everything she had kept locked away. She could almost hear his voice, his excuses, but it didn't matter. The fantasy felt good. It felt right.

As much as she tried to bury it, she couldn't ignore the jealousy that burned within her. Her so-called friends, family members, including her cousins, the ones who always seemed to have something to say, always judging her from the sidelines, envying her beauty, her strength. They didn't know the real her. They didn't know the pain that festered beneath the surface.

"They think they know me," she sneered, the words leaving her lips like venom. "But they have no idea."

She could feel the resentment growing, bubbling up from deep within. It was a part of her now, just as much as the peace she had found in the woods. The wilderness had become her sanctuary, but it had also given her the space to confront the darkness that still lived within her.

But, for now, she pushed those thoughts aside. For now, she allowed herself to bask in the quiet, in the beauty of the forest that surrounded her.

She smiled as she watched the last remnants of daylight fade into the night sky, the stars twinkling overhead like a million tiny promises. "This is enough," she whispered softly to herself. "This is the life I've chosen."

Her heart swelled with a sense of contentment, as if the universe had finally conspired to give her this moment of peace. The road ahead was unclear, but in this moment, everything felt right. The wilderness had healed her in ways she hadn't even realized she needed. It had taught her how to be still, how to listen to the world around her, and, most importantly, how to listen to herself.

"Maybe this is what I've always needed," she thought, her eyes closing as the night settled around her. "Maybe this is the peace I've been searching for."

And for a fleeting moment, she truly believed it.

But even as the peacefulness enveloped her, there was still a lingering darkness, a shadow that followed her wherever she went. It was the reality of her journey. The wilderness had been her teacher, her protector, but it hadn't changed the fact that she was running from something. From someone. There would be no real peace until she had made peace with herself and with the people who had wronged her. Until then, the weight of the past shadowed her every step, like a ghost that refused to rest.

Seven took one last look at the stars, taking a deep breath before settling down for the night. As she drifted off to sleep, she couldn't shake the feeling that this was only the beginning. She had made a choice, and that choice would shape her future in ways she couldn't yet understand. But for now, she was content, her heart heavy with the lessons she had learned and the road that lay ahead.

14

The Edge of Everything

T he stars above were merciless in their beauty, a stark contrast to the turmoil brewing inside Seven. The stillness of the wilderness enveloped her, the forest breathing softly around her as if it held secrets she wasn't ready to uncover. Her body ached from the weight of exhaustion, and the cold ground beneath her seeped into her bones. She curled onto her side, her head resting against her makeshift pillow, trying to focus on the serenity of the night.

But the peace she longed for remained elusive.

Sleep came reluctantly, not as a comfort but as a surrender dragging her under like a tide she could no longer resist.

Run

Seven was running.

Her bare feet pounded against the unyielding ground, each jarring step reverberating through her bones. The air hung heavy and suffocating, thick with the weight of something unseen. Around her, the world morphed into a grotesque, ever-shifting maze. Jagged trees with gnarled, skeletal branches clawed at the kaleidoscopic sky, which swirled in unnatural hues of black and crimson. Shadows slithered across the landscape like oil spilled on water, moving with a life of their own.

Something was chasing her.

She could feel it an overwhelming presence closing in, its malevolence tangible in the air. The sound of its pursuit was everywhere: the guttural growls of beasts that shouldn't exist, the rhythmic pounding of distorted footsteps that echoed endlessly, and an unearthly, high-pitched whine that drilled into her skull.

"Help!" Seven screamed, her voice raw with desperation. But the world around her swallowed the sound, muting her cries as if mocking her helplessness.

She didn't dare look back.

Her lungs burned, her legs felt like lead, and every breath scraped painfully against her throat. Ahead of her, the ground seemed to stretch infinitely, but its shape was wrong—twisting and contorting as if alive. Forests bled into barren fields, fields melted into crumbling cities, and the sky dissolved into a smothering black void. Reality itself unraveled with every frantic step.

The creatures chasing her multiplied. What had started as one shadow had split into countless forms, their peculiar outlines rippling and merging like a nightmarish dance of smoke and flesh.

A moment of weakness overtook her, and she dared to glance back.

Her heart stopped.

The figures were unlike anything human. Their strange forms were humanoid, but distorted and exaggerated. Their limbs stretched and twisted unnaturally, their joints bending in impossible directions. Eyes glowed a hellish red, unblinking and piercing, while their faces contorted into grins that were too wide, too jagged, revealing uneven rows of sharp, mismatched teeth.

They moved with an unnatural speed, their jerky, marionette-like motions somehow faster than her frantic sprint. Their hands, long and clawed, reached out, grasping at the air between them and her.

Seven's chest heaved as panic took hold. Her feet barely skimmed the uneven ground as she pushed herself harder, faster.

"Leave me alone!" she screamed, her voice cracking.

The creatures didn't stop. They didn't need to respond; their silence spoke louder than words. The unrelenting chase, the inevitability of their pursuit, was the true terror.

Up ahead, the ground transformed again. This time, it split violently, revealing a chasm so deep and dark it seemed to devour the surrounding light. Seven skidded to a halt at the edge, her arms pinwheeling for balance. Below her, the abyss stretched endlessly, its depths a void that seemed alive, breathing, calling to her.

Her heart thundered as she teetered on the brink, her body shaking with the effort to stay upright. She turned her head slightly, just enough to see the creatures advancing. They had paused, their grotesque forms frozen for a brief, agonizing moment. Their eyes, glowing like embers, locked onto her with a predatory hunger.

They knew there was nowhere for her to go.

"No," Seven whispered, her voice trembling. Her feet shuffled backward instinctively, but the edge crumbled beneath her heel. "No, no, no!"

The creatures lunged as one, their movements synchronized like a horrifying swarm.

Seven screamed, her voice raw and ragged, as her body plunged into the abyss.

The fall was endless.

Her stomach lurched as gravity tore her downward, the air rushing past her in a deafening roar. She flailed wildly, her limbs useless against the void that consumed her. Above her, the creatures followed, their forms blurring and merging into one massive shadow that seemed to devour the darkness itself.

The entity expanded, its shape writhing and shifting like a living storm. Faces appeared and disappeared within its form—screaming, laughing, snarling. The weight of its presence pressed against her from all sides, suffocating and inescapable.

"Please!" Seven begged, though she didn't know who or what she was pleading with.

The darkness closed in, growing thicker, heavier, until she could no longer tell where her body ended and the void began. The sensation of falling morphed into something worse, something she couldn't define but could feel in every fiber of her being.

And then, just as the void threatened to swallow her whole, Seven hit the ground with a bone-jarring impact.

The world around her shattered like glass, fragments of light and shadow spiraling away into nothingness.

Awake

Her eyes flew open, her chest heaving as she gasped for air. The stars above blurred and twisted, her vision swimming as she tried to ground herself. Her hands gripped the earth beneath her, the cool dirt a stark contrast to the heat that radiated from her clammy skin.

Seven sat up abruptly, her heart racing as if it were trying to escape her chest. She pressed a trembling hand to her forehead, wiping away the sweat that dripped down her face.

"It was just a dream," she whispered hoarsely, though the words felt hollow.

"It wasn't real," she repeated to herself, the words a weak attempt at reassurance. But the memory of the dream refused to fade.

The sensation of falling, the glowing eyes, the sickening grins. It was all still there, etched into her mind like a brand.

Seven glanced at the horizon, where the first hints of dawn began to seep into the sky. The soft, warm hues of morning light felt like a balm to her frayed nerves, but the unease lingered.

The dream had been a warning. She didn't know what it meant, but she couldn't ignore the feeling that it had tried to tell her something. Something she wasn't ready to face.

Her body betrayed her, every nerve on edge, every breath labored. The memory of the dream clung to her like a second skin, the sensation of falling still alive in her gut. She glanced around the clearing, half-expecting to see the shadows lurking in the trees.

But there was nothing. Only the whisper of the wind and the faint rustle of leaves.

Seven drew her knees to her chest, wrapping her arms around them as she tried to calm the storm raging inside her. She took slow, deliberate breaths, each one a small rebellion against the terror that threatened to consume her.

A New Morning

When dawn broke, the forest felt different. The golden light filtered through the canopy, casting everything in a warm glow that seemed to push back the darkness of the night before. Seven rose slowly, her muscles stiff and her mind still clouded with the remnants of the dream.

The world around her felt alive in a way she hadn't noticed before. The hum of insects, the distant call of birds, the gentle rustling of leaves; it all felt amplified, as if the forest itself was breathing with her.

She walked aimlessly, letting the sounds and sights of nature guide her. Her steps were slow and intentional, her senses attuned to every detail. She watched as a butterfly danced from one flower to the next, its delicate wings catching the morning light. She saw a line of ants marching with precision, each one carrying a burden far heavier than itself.

For the first time in days, Seven felt a strange sense of connection to the world, to herself, to something greater.

Reflection

As she sat by a meandering creek, her thoughts drifted to the dream. The shadows, the chase, the fall—it all felt symbolic, though she couldn't quite piece together what it meant.

"Maybe it's everything I've been running from," she murmured, her voice barely audible above the sound of the water. "Maybe it's everything I'm afraid to face."

Seven dipped her fingers into the cool water, watching as the ripples spread outward in perfect circles. "I can't keep running," she said to herself, the words feeling both heavy and freeing.

Immersed in Nature

The day unfolded with a surreal quality, each moment imbued with a sense of purpose she couldn't quite explain. She found herself drawn to the smallest details; the way the sunlight played on the surface of the water, the way the wind whispered through the trees, the way the earth felt solid beneath her feet.

She followed a deer for a while, its graceful movements mesmerizing. It led her to a meadow filled with wildflowers, their vibrant colors a stark contrast to the muted tones of the forest. Seven knelt among the flowers, her hands brushing against their soft petals.

For the first time, she felt a sense of peace, not the fleeting kind she had chased her entire life, but something deeper, something rooted in the present moment.

As the sun dipped below the horizon, painting the sky in hues of orange and pink, Seven sat alone in the meadow. The memory of the dream still lingered, but it no longer felt like a threat. It felt like a challenge, and a reminder that she was still standing, still fighting, still moving forward.

She wasn't afraid of the edge.

She was ready to confront it.

15

Strange Encounter

Seven rose from the meadow, the soft petals brushing her hands. The sky blazed with the last light of day, warm and golden, as if the forest itself were offering a quiet benediction.

For a few moments, she simply stood there, breathing in the wild scents of earth and grass, feeling the steady pulse of life beneath her feet. The peace she'd found wasn't fleeting—it felt rooted deep inside, like a fragile seed ready to grow.

But as the shadows lengthened, a whisper of doubt crept into her mind—subtle, insistent.

This place, beautiful and alive as it was, it wasn't reality. It was a pause, a sanctuary carved out from the chaos of her life. And while she could rest here, she knew she couldn't stay.

Her heart tightened with a quiet ache, a reminder that the world outside the forest still waited, with all its dangers and demands of its own.

Seven took a steadying breath, her gaze drifting toward the darkening tree line ahead.

"I can't stay here," she whispered, voice steady but heavy with meaning. "Not forever."

Seven's breath came slower now, measured, almost steady. But beneath the surface, her stomach churned with unease. The forest stretched on, a labyrinth of identical trunks and tangled undergrowth, endless and unforgiving. Each step seemed to carry her in circles, a cruel maze with no exit.

She had always prided herself on resilience, on grit that could bend but never break. Yet here, in this shadowed wilderness, that confidence faltered. The air was thick and heavy, moisture clinging to her skin, but her throat burned dry. Her lungs fought for each ragged breath, her body taut with exhaustion.

The dead phone weighing against her hip felt like a cruel reminder — her last link to the world beyond this tangled green prison was gone. Now she was utterly alone. Alone with the relentless silence, alone with the slow gnawing panic that edged her thoughts.

Then, cutting through the stillness, a sharp, piercing cry split the air.

Seven froze. Her gaze snapped upward, tracing the silhouette of an eagle gliding high above the treetops. Its wings caught the fading light, sharp and commanding against the dusk. The wild call echoed through the trees, both beautiful and unnerving.

The eagle circled, watching her with keen, unblinking eyes. Seven's heart thudded as a strange chill trickled down her spine, like the bird carried a silent message she couldn't yet understand.

A sudden pang in her chest brought her back, not to the present, but to another time.

The air shifted, and her senses blurred as her mind pulled her into a memory.

A Flash of Memory

She was eight years old, running through the woods with her cousins, Malik and Jessie. The three of them had discovered a small clearing near their aunt's house that summer, an untouched patch of wilderness that became their playground. Seven could still hear their laughter as it echoed through her mind, bright and carefree, unburdened by the weight of the world they hadn't yet come to understand.

Malik, always the bold one, brandished a stick like it was Excalibur, slicing the air with wild swings. Jada, younger and smaller, scampered after him, giggling as she waved a crooked branch she'd claimed as her magic wand. Seven trailed behind them, breathing in the crisp air, carefree and full of wonder.

"Last one to the tree's a rotten egg!" Malik shouted, his voice ringing out like a challenge.

"No fair!" Jada protested, but she darted forward, her little legs pumping with everything she had.

Seven remembered the way the earth felt beneath her sandals, solid and dependable, and the way the sunlight streamed through the branches, painting the forest floor in dappled patches of gold. The three of them played until their aunt's distant call reminded them the streetlights would soon turn on, signaling the end of their adventures for the day.

It was the kind of childhood memory that lived deep in her bones, a snapshot of pure joy. Yet it was laced with a bittersweet ache now. Both Malik and Jessie were gone, their lives cut tragically short before they'd had the chance to grow into the remarkable people she'd always believed they'd become.

A Spiritual Connection

The memory washed over her like a wave, leaving Seven rooted in place. She closed her eyes, and for a brief moment, she swore she could hear their voices again, faint and fleeting, like the wind whispering through the trees.

"I hope you both know I love you," she whispered to the forest, to her cousins, to the spirits she felt lingering just out of reach.

The eagle cried out again, its sharp call jolting her back to the present. Seven opened her eyes, tears spilling unbidden down her cheeks. She wiped them away quickly, as though ashamed to show even the forest her vulnerability.

If Malik and Jessie were here, she thought, they wouldn't be running. They wouldn't see this forest as a trap, as a maze to escape. They would see it for what it was: a playground, a sanctuary, a place to live freely and fully, something she felt at times, however those moments were fleeting.

Her lips curled into a faint smile as she thought of Malik daring her to climb the tallest tree or Jessie crowning herself queen of the forest with a crown of leaves. They had always pushed the limits, testing how far they could go before the streetlights came on and they were forced to return home.

Seven let out a shaky breath. "I think you had it figured out," she said softly. "It's not about running away, is it? It's about choosing to live."

For the first time since she'd entered the forest, Seven felt something shift inside her. The wilderness wasn't her enemy. It wasn't a place to escape or fear. It was a reflection of her own soul—chaotic and wild, yes, but also beautiful and alive.

She took another step forward, her footing surer now, her breaths deeper. She didn't know where she was going, but she was determined to find out.

A Cry from Above

A sudden, piercing cry shattered the oppressive silence, sending a jolt of adrenaline coursing through her veins. Seven chilled, her head jolted upward to locate the source.

That same eagle. It soared high above the treetops, its wings outstretched in a majestic display of power and grace. The sight was both fascinating and distracting. The bird circled her, its sharp cry cutting through the dense air like a warning.

Seven watched in awe as the eagle glided effortlessly, its sharp talons glinting faintly in the dim light. For a moment, the bird locked eyes with her, and she felt an inexplicable connection.

"What are you trying to tell me?" she muttered, her voice barely above a whisper.

The eagle let out another subtle cry before banking sharply and disappearing behind a cluster of trees. Seven's shoulders slumped as the weight of her situation settled back onto her chest.

"Get a grip," she told herself, shaking her head. "It's just a bird."

But deep down, she couldn't shake the feeling that the eagle's presence meant something.

The Watchful Figure

As she trudged forward, the oppressive silence returned, broken only by the occasional rustle of leaves or snap of a twig. Each sound set her on edge, her heart pounding with every step.

Then, through the tangled web of branches, she saw him.

He leaned casually against a massive tree, his posture relaxed but his presence commanding. His clothes were tattered and patched, a quilt of survival stitched together with necessity. His dark eyes locked onto hers, unblinking and intense.

Seven's breath caught in her throat. The man didn't belong here—at least, not in the way she did. He seemed to be a part of the forest, as though he had grown from the very earth itself.

"You look lost," he said, his voice low and gravelly.

Seven's instinct was to run, but her legs wouldn't obey. She squared her shoulders, masking her fear with a glare. "I'm fine," she replied, her voice sharper than she intended.

The man smirked, his dark eyes glinting with amusement. "Fine?" he repeated, pushing off the tree. "You don't look fine. You look like someone who's just realized they're in over their head."

"I don't need your help," Seven snapped, taking a step back.

"Help?" He chuckled, the sound deep and unsettling. "Funny thing about people who say they don't need help, they're usually the ones who need it most."

Cryptic Connections

Seven's frustration boiled over, her exhaustion and fear bubbling to the surface. "I just need to find my car," she said, her voice trembling slightly. "If you will not help me, then leave me alone."

The man tilted his head, studying her like a puzzle he was trying to piece together. "Your car," he said slowly, as if tasting the words. "And where do you think you're going once you find it?"

"Away from here," Seven snapped, her patience wearing thin.

The man's smirk widened, but his eyes remained cold. "Away from here," he repeated mockingly. "Sounds like a solid plan."

Seven's jaw tightened, her hands balling into fists at her sides. "Listen, I don't know why you insist on speaking to me. You don't know me and I am not open to getting to know you."

"Hey, I'm just trying to have a friendly conversation?" His voice was soft, almost taunting. "I'm just saying nobody ends up in a place like this by accident. The forest has a way of drawing in people who've got nowhere else to go."

Seven opened her mouth to retort, but his words hit too close to home. She looked away, her silence speaking volumes.

"Just leave me alone," Seven said, her voice trembling, "I don't owe you an explanation."

"You're right," he said, his voice softening. "You don't. But maybe you owe one to yourself."

Collapse

The man's words echoed in Seven's mind as she pushed past him, her steps quickening as she plunged deeper into the forest.

"Running won't fix anything!" he called after her, his voice following her like a shadow. "You can't outrun yourself!"

His words struck a nerve, but Seven refused to acknowledge them. She focused on putting as much distance between them as possible, her breaths coming in short, ragged gasps.

Above her, the eagle appeared again, its abrupt cry cutting through the thick air. Seven glanced up, her vision blurring as exhaustion took hold.

"I just need to keep going," she whispered, her voice barely audible. But her body had other plans. Her legs buckled, and she collapsed onto the cold, unforgiving ground.

A Stranger's Help

When Seven awoke, the world was a haze of muted colors and muffled sounds. Her body ached, and her head throbbed with a dull, persistent pain.

"Hey," a voice said softly, pulling her from the fog.

Seven blinked, her vision clearing to reveal a man crouched beside her. He had a rugged appearance, his face weathered by the elements, but his eyes were kind and concerned.

"You okay?" he asked, his tone gentle.

Seven tried to sit up, wincing as her muscles protested. "Who are you?"

"Just a fellow wanderer," he replied with a faint smile. "Even though you took off, I found you lying here and thought you could use a hand."

Seven's gaze flicked to the surrounding forest, her memory piecing itself together. "I was... I was looking for my car."

The man nodded. "You're not the first person to get turned around out here."

Something about his presence became oddly calming, despite the surreal nature of the encounter. Seven allowed herself to relax slightly, though her guard remained up.

"Where am I?" she asked, her voice barely above a whisper.

The man's expression softened. "You're in the middle of nowhere, honestly. But you're not alone."

Seven frowned, his words both reassuring and unsettling. She glanced up, and the eagle's cry echoed a sharp reminder of the strange journey that had brought her here.

16

Are you Awake

Seven's eyelids fluttered, heavy with exhaustion, her mind sluggish as reality seeped in like a creeping fog. She felt the chill of damp soil pressing through her clothes, unyielding and cold against her back. The air smelled of smoke and pine, mingled with the sharper scent of burning wood. Shadows danced across her closed eyes, patterns that seemed alive and deliberate.

The warmth of the fire, close yet distant, hummed with a strange, hypnotic pull. It crackled softly, each pop and hiss sending tiny embers into the night sky, dissolving into the nothingness beyond. Her body ached as if the earth had bruised her itself, but it was a deeper, unexplainable weariness—a weariness that came from something beyond the physical.

She forced her eyes open, and the orange glow of the campfire blazed against the dark, its flames licking the night air. Shapes flickered and twisted in the flames, casting erratic light onto the forest floor. Her muscles protested as she tried to move, her limbs stiff and weak, a body that felt like it was no longer fully hers.

Her breath caught in her throat when a voice pierced the stillness. It was low, guttural, and so matter-of-fact that it sent a jolt through her spine.

"See how things turn out when you think you know it all? Passed out in the middle of nowhere. With strangers."

Her heart thudded painfully against her ribs, and her hand flew to her necklace, clutching the pendant like a talisman. The cool, smooth metal grounded her as her eyes darted toward the source of the voice. Across the fire, a man sat casually against a tree, poking at the flames with a stick. His face, partially illuminated by the fire, was rugged and lined with years of hardship. His expression was one of mocking amusement, the corners of his lips twitching upwards in a way that felt unnervingly familiar.

"What... what are you doing to me?" Seven croaked, her throat dry, the words scratching at her like sandpaper.

The man snorted, his lips curling into a smirk. "'What are you doing to me?'" he mimicked, exaggerating her tone like a child mocking a sibling. Then he let out a low, throaty laugh, shaking his head. "Lady, you're the one who passed out in the middle of nowhere. You're lucky I found you before something else did."

Seven struggled to sit up, her body trembling with the effort. Every movement felt like fighting against her own weakness. "I don't trust you," she snapped, her voice gaining a little more strength as she pushed herself into a sitting position, the ground cold beneath her.

The man raised an eyebrow, his smirk widening. "Trust me? That's cute. Listen, if I wanted to hurt you, I wouldn't have waited for you to wake up. You're not exactly in a position to fight me off." He reached for a tin cup sitting near the fire and held it out to her. "Here. Water. You look like you need it."

Seven stared at the cup, suspicion etched into every line of her face. Every part of her screamed to avoid the offer, to turn and run, but exhaustion crept in deeper, her throat burning with thirst.

"Oh, for crying out loud," the man said, rolling his eyes. "You think I poisoned it? Young lady, I don't need to spike your drink. I'm twice your size, and you're already half-dead from whatever it is you're running from. Just take it."

Her throat burned with thirst, and despite her better judgment, she reached for the cup. Her fingers brushed against his, rough and calloused, as she took it. The water was lukewarm but soothing, quenching the dryness in her mouth and throat. She drank deeply before handing the cup back.

"Better?" he asked, leaning back against the tree trunk, his tone casual, as though they were old friends sharing a campfire.

Seven said nothing, her eyes fixed on the fire. Her mind raced, the heat from the flames juxtaposed with the chill creeping up her spine from the stranger's unnerving presence. Despite the warmth, a coldness lingered, one that seeped into her bones with every passing second.

"Now," the man said, his voice turning serious, "let's get to the real question. What the hell are you doing out here?"

Seven's hand instinctively tightened around her necklace. She pulled her knees closer to her chest, trying to shrink into herself. "I don't have to tell you anything," she said, her tone defensive, brittle, like a thin sheet of ice.

"You don't," he agreed with a shrug. "But you're in my woods now, and I haven't had anyone to talk to in years. So, humor me. Amuse me, and maybe I'll help you find your car."

Seven let out a bitter laugh, shaking her head. "You think this is funny? I don't even know your name."

"Names don't matter out here," he said, his voice calm, even. "What matters is why you're running."

"I'm not running," she blurted, her voice defensive, sharper than she intended.

"Sure you're not," he replied, his smirk returning. "You think I haven't seen your type before? People don't end up out here by accident. So, what is it? Bad breakup? Family drama? Or maybe..." He paused, tilting his head, his eyes glinting in the firelight. "Maybe you just couldn't handle the weight of your own expectations."

Seven's hands balled into fists. "You don't know anything about me."

"Don't I?" he said, his voice soft but cutting. "You wouldn't be here if everything was fine. Nobody ends up in a place like this if everything is fine."

She opened her mouth to retort, but his words hit too close to home. Instead, she glared at him, her silence speaking volumes.

The man nodded slowly, as if her silence confirmed something he already knew. "That's what I thought. You've been carrying a lot, haven't you? Too much, maybe."

"Stop," she said, her voice trembling as she tried to hold her ground, the weight of his words sinking in.

"Why?" He spread his arms wide, his expression almost taunting. "Isn't that why you're here? To face whatever's been eating away at you?"

"No," she snapped. "I'm here because..." she trailed off, her throat tightening as she couldn't form the words.

"Because why?" he pressed. Was it because the world became too difficult? Did someone hurt you? Because you think disappearing will make it all go away?

Seven took a step back, her breath hitching. "I don't owe you an explanation."

"You're right," he said, his tone softening. "You don't. But maybe you owe one to yourself."

They stood in silence for a moment, the forest eerily still. Seven's mind raced, the man's words digging into places she didn't want to examine.

"Nice bracelet," he said suddenly, breaking the silence.

She blinked, caught off guard. "What?"

He gestured to her wrist. "Your bracelet. It's nice. Expensive, I bet."

She instinctively covered it with her hand. "It was a gift."

"From who?"

"My dad." Her voice was quieter now, tinged with a mix of defensiveness and nostalgia.

"Must be a hell of a dad to give you something like that," the man said, his tone unreadable.

Seven let out a bitter laugh. "Hardly. It's just his way of making up for lost time."

The man's expression shifted, a flicker of something softer crossing his face. "At least he did something. Some of us get nothing."

She frowned, his words cutting deeper than she expected. "Yeah, well, a nice bracelet doesn't fix everything."

"No, it doesn't," he agreed. "But it's something. And something's better than nothing."

Seven shifted uncomfortably, unsure how to respond. The man's presence unsettled her, but there was something about him—something raw and unfiltered—that felt oddly familiar.

"Why are you even out here?" she asked, desperate to turn the conversation away from herself.

"Same reason as you, I guess," he said, resting against a tree. "Trying to make sense of things... running from the noise. Only I got caught in it. Stuck. Not because I can't leave—but because I don't know who I'd be if I did. I tell myself I'm part of the wilderness now, like I belong to it... but truth is, I wouldn't even know how to go back if I tried. And maybe that's what scares me most—that I want to, but it's already too late."

"Escape from what?"

"Life," he said simply. "People. Expectations. Sometimes, it's easier to be out here, where the only thing you have to answer to is the land."

Seven tilted her head, studying him. "And does it work? Does being in the space of the wilderness help you find the answers?"

He met her gaze, his eyes dark and intense. "No. But it gives you space to think. To figure out what really matters."

Seven hesitated, his words striking a chord she didn't want to acknowledge. "I just want to find my car and leave," she said finally. "Can you help me or not?"

The man smirked. "Not."

She threw up her hands in frustration. "Seriously? My phone is dead, and I'm lost! Are you really just going to stand there and let me wander around aimlessly?"

"Pretty much," he said with a shrug.

"You're unbelievable," she muttered, turning to walk away.

"Where do you think you're going?" he called after her.

"To find my car!"

"And then what?" he shouted, his voice echoing through the trees. "You think you can outrun yourself, little girl? You think the road will magically solve all your problems?"

Seven ignored him, her steps growing quicker as she moved deeper into the forest.

"You're scared!" he yelled, his voice chasing after her like a shadow. "Scared of life, scared of yourself. That's why you're out here. Running won't change that!"

His words echoed in her mind long after his voice faded into the distance.

Hours passed, or maybe it was minutes—time felt meaningless in the darkness. Seven's legs grew weaker, her breaths more labored. The forest seemed to stretch endlessly, each tree mocking her with its sameness.

Her vision blurred, her body swaying as exhaustion took hold. She thought of Ryan, her heart aching with a longing so profound it nearly brought her to her knees.

"I'm sorry, Ryan," she whispered, her voice barely audible. "I just wanted to be enough."

The world tilted, the edges of her vision darkening. And then, like a marionette whose strings had been cut, she collapsed, the cold earth rising to meet her.

17

Journey Back

S even tightened her grip on the steering wheel, the hum of the car's engine steady as it carried her along the winding road. The towering trees on either side seemed to close in, their shadows stretching across the asphalt like reaching hands. The rain from earlier had cleared, leaving the road slick and shimmering under the glow of her headlights.

Her chest rose and fell with a deep sigh, her mind tangled in thoughts she couldn't untangle. Every mile brought her closer to home, to Ryan, to the life she'd fled from in a storm of emotions. Yet, with each passing moment, the weight of her return pressed down on her, heavy and relentless.

Her mind wandered. Ryan's laugh came first, bright and uncontainable. Seven could almost hear it, the way it filled a room with joy. She pictured her daughter's mischievous grin, her small hands tugging on Seven's shirt, demanding her attention. "Mommy, mommy, mommy! I wanna play!"

Seven's lips curved into a faint smile, though her chest ached with longing.

Her thoughts shifted to her mother's kitchen, the aroma of sweet potato pie wafting from the oven. She imagined leaning against the counter, sneaking spoonfuls of the sugary filling when her mom wasn't looking. Her stomach growled at the memory, and she let out a small chuckle.

Her brothers, Kase and Karter, appeared next in her mind. Kase's voice was loud and teasing, as it always was. "What the hell were you thinking, Seven? Are you on that stuff?" His exaggerated tone and wide grin were so vivid she almost laughed aloud.

But it was Karter, her youngest brother, who brought a distinct warmth to her heart. Their bond had always been special, quieter but no less deep. She thought of the time they sat down together to write a song, a simple idea that turned into something beautiful because of Karter's meticulous attention to detail.

"Hold on, pause right here, Sev," Karter had said, his voice gentle, the way it always got when he was deep in thought. He leaned over her shoulder, tapping the page softly with his pen. "Let the silence carry it for a second. That way, when you bring it back in… it won't just be words. It'll mean something."

She could still see the way his eyes lit up when they played the finished song back to themselves. He'd always had a way of turning simple moments into something profound.

Seven sighed, her fingers brushing against the pendant around her neck. She wondered if Karter missed her as much as she missed him.

Her thoughts expanded further, weaving through her favorite memories of family gatherings. Her aunts' laughter echoed in her mind, loud and infectious, as they played cards at the dining room table. Seven could picture her aunt slapping down a winning card with triumphant glee, her laughter filling the room.

The sound of children's giggles came next, her nieces and nephews running through the house with uncontainable energy. Seven smiled at the memory of their tiny feet racing across the floor, their joy infectious and grounding.

For a fleeting moment, it all felt so real. Seven could almost reach out and touch it—the warmth, the chaos, the love that had always made her feel whole.

But reality crept back in, cold and unyielding. The road ahead stretched into the darkness, endless and uncertain. Seven exhaled deeply, letting the memories settle like leaves floating to the ground.

The static from the radio filled the car as she adjusted the station, scrolling through frequencies in search of something to break the silence. Even the white noise felt comforting, a familiar backdrop to her restless thoughts. She twisted the dial, glancing down for just a moment.

When she looked back up, her breath hitched.

A deer stood in the middle of the road, its wide eyes reflecting the headlights like twin mirrors.

"Shit!" Seven screamed, yanking the wheel to the side.

The tires screeched, and the car skidded violently, veering off the road. The right side of the vehicle slammed into a tree with a sickening crunch, the force jerking her forward against the seatbelt. Steam hissed from the hood, curling into the cool night air.

For a moment, everything was still.

Seven sat frozen, her breath shallow and rapid. Her hands clutched the steering wheel, her knuckles white with tension. Slowly, she raised a trembling hand to her face, feeling for any injuries. Her fingers brushed against her forehead and cheeks—no blood, just clammy skin.

She unbuckled her seatbelt and pushed the door open, stumbling out into the cool night. The air smelled damp, earthy, and metallic, the sharp scent of the accident mingling with the faint aroma of rain.

The deer was still there, standing a few feet away. Its silhouette was bathed in the faint glow of the headlights, its dark eyes unblinking and calm.

Seven's breath caught. The animal seemed to be watching her, studying her.

"What the hell..." she whispered, her voice shaky.

The deer turned slowly, its movements deliberate. Its hooves clicked softly against the wet asphalt as it walked down the center of the road, disappearing into the shadows.

Turning back to the car, Seven crouched to inspect the damage. The hood was crumpled, steam hissing from the cracked radiator. She knelt down, peering underneath to check for leaks. The sight of the bent metal made her stomach churn.

"Shit," she muttered, standing up and kicking a small rock in frustration.

Rain began to fall again, softly at first, then heavier. Seven climbed back into the car, slamming the door behind her. She grabbed her jacket from the passenger seat and wrapped it around herself, shivering as the cold seeped in.

Her eyes flicked to the rearview mirror, half-expecting to see the deer standing there again. But the road behind her was empty, the darkness unbroken.

She leaned back in her seat, her head resting against the cushion. "What the hell, Seven? I've gotta get back to work. I've gotta get back to Ryan."

Her fingers tightened around the edges of her jacket as she adjusted her seat. The rain pattered against the roof, its steady rhythm soothing and relentless. Exhaustion pulled at her, and her eyes fluttered closed.

Her thoughts drifted in and out, memories swirling like leaves caught in a storm.

"Mommy, mommy, mommy! I wanna play!"

Ryan's sweet voice echoed in her mind, pulling at her heart with tiny, invisible hands.

"Seven, you only got the promotion because the boss thinks you're cute. Doesn't make you better for the job."

The biting words of her co-worker cut through her, sharp and cold.

Her father's voice followed, softer but tinged with regret. "I know I haven't been the greatest dad, but I do love you."

Then Michael's voice drifted in, soft but razor-edged: "I'm sorry, Seven, but is this where you bring up commitment again? Where you remind me how long we've been doing this and how I should've figured it out by now?"

Her mother's voice came next, stern and unwavering: "Seven, you have a great life. You need to be more grateful."

Finally, Kase's teasing voice rang out, mocking and loud: "You're a spoiled brat, Seven. The world doesn't revolve around you."

The voices grew louder, overlapping in a cacophony that made her chest tighten. Seven stirred, clutching the edges of her jacket as though it could shield her from the storm raging inside her mind.

The rain fell harder; the sound growing more intense as the drops pelted the roof. Seven's breathing slowed, her chest rising and falling as exhaustion finally claimed her.

She drifted into a restless sleep; her dreams a kaleidoscope of fragmented memories and haunting whispers.

"Why are you running?"

The voice was deep and unfamiliar, cutting through the chaos like a blade. Seven turned in her dream, searching for its source.

"You can't run forever."

The voice echoed, growing louder, closer. Seven's pulse quickened, and she spun around, her breath coming in shallow gasps.

"Face it."

The whisper was barely audible, but it sent a shiver down her spine.

Seven jolted awake, her heart racing and her breath ragged. The rain had stopped, leaving the world outside eerily quiet. She sat there, staring into the darkness, the remnants of the dream clinging to her like cobwebs.

For the first time, the thought of going home felt like more than an obligation. It felt like salvation.

18

A Change in Perspective

S even woke slowly, the soft hum of her car's engine reverberating through her body. The sunlight that filtered through the trees outside the car window was gentle, casting a soft glow over everything. The rain had ceased, leaving only the faint smell of damp earth and the cool morning air to greet her.

It felt as though the world had paused, time itself holding its breath, just long enough for her to catch hers. The hush that followed was more than quiet; it was soothing, like nature pressing a cool hand to her fevered thoughts.

She rubbed her eyes and stretched her arms above her head, the stiff muscles in her back protesting, but she didn't mind. Every ache and stiffness felt grounding, like a reminder that she had been through something. She had been through a journey, and though it wasn't over, she was closer to finding herself.

The question she had asked herself last night surfaced again. Why had she been running for so long? Not just mentally, from the memories she buried and the truths she refused to face, but eventually physically too, the weight of it all leading her to the wild. The escape became literal only after the emotional turmoil reached its breaking point. And now something was shifting. That quiet pull again. A gentle urging to return, not just from the forest's edge, but from the tangled, unspoken places inside her. It was as if an invisible thread had been tugging at her chest, guiding her back not only to where she came from, but to who she was becoming.

With a deep sigh, Seven started the car and pulled onto the road. The path ahead was still unclear, but as her tires rolled smoothly over the damp pavement, she found a kind of comfort in the rhythm. It felt like she was being guided.

Her fingers lightly gripped the steering wheel, and with every passing mile, the fog in her mind seemed to clear, even if just a little. The trees lining the road were taller now, their trunks thick and gnarled. The light filtering through their branches seemed to bathe everything in a gold-green glow. A kind of peace settled over her as she drove, as if she had stepped into another world, one where everything was connected.

Rusty's Mart emerged through the thinning trees, its faded sign creaking on rusted hinges above the door. Although it had only been a brief stop on her way into the woods, the sight of it now struck her with unexpected force. The weathered building, surrounded by cracked pavement and wild grass, felt like more than just a convenience store. It was a threshold, a quiet and unassuming marker of where she had been and how far she had come. This place reminded her that the journey back had already begun.

Pulling into the gravel parking lot, Seven turned off the engine. The store looked exactly the same as it had yesterday, but there was a strange feeling in the air today. A feeling like something was about to shift. It was as if the universe had paused again, waiting for her to take the next step.

She stepped out of the car, the cool breeze ruffling her hair as she walked toward the door. The bell above the entrance chimed softly as she entered. Behind the counter stood the clerk, the same woman from days before. Her eyes flickered up to meet Seven's, and she gave a soft smile, her face lighting up with recognition.

"Well, well, well, look who's back," the clerk said with a knowing smile. There was something about her presence that felt otherworldly, as if she had seen things Seven couldn't even imagine. "I was wondering when you'd return."

Seven paused for a moment, the weight of her own emotions pressing down on her. She hadn't realized how much she needed this moment, this space. "I wasn't planning on coming back," Seven said quietly, the words spilling out. "But something about today... something felt different. I needed to stop. I needed to understand."

The clerk raised an eyebrow, her gaze piercing but kind. "I've learned that sometimes the universe pulls us in ways we can't fully understand. It makes little sense at first. But when you let it take you somewhere, when you let it unfold... that's when the magic happens."

Seven's heart skipped a beat. *Magic?* The word wasn't unfamiliar. It echoed something she already believed in, in her own way. Signs. Synchronicities. The quiet guidance of something greater. But hearing it spoken aloud, so boldly and without hesitation, stirred something deeper. It wasn't just the word. It was the weight behind it, the quiet certainty in the woman's voice. There was something about her, something timeworn yet steady with wisdom, that made Seven pause.

This didn't feel like coincidence. It felt like another thread in the pattern she was just beginning to see.

"What do you mean?" Seven asked, her voice softer now. "What magic?"

The clerk's lips curled into a half-smile and she took a step forward. "Magic is all around us. It's in the way the world shifts when we shift our perspective. The way we can stop seeing everything as obstacles and start seeing them as lessons, signs, and gifts from the universe. You're running from things, but what if the universe is giving you exactly what you need in ways you're not prepared to see?" Her voice wasn't pushy or overly mystical, just calm and knowing. Seven looked at her more closely, not just as the odd woman behind the counter, but as someone who had clearly weathered her own storms. There was something about the woman's stillness, her quiet conviction, that made Seven wonder how many paths had led her here to Rusty's Mart. Maybe she had her own stories buried deep, her own kind of wisdom earned the hard way.

Seven stood still, her eyes wide as she took in the clerk's words. The weight of her journey, the pain, the fears, the disappointment, suddenly felt lighter. But there was still something nagging at her, something she didn't fully understand.

She reached out and picked up a Lucky 7 lottery ticket from the counter, her fingers brushing lightly against the faded paper. It was a random act, but somehow, in the quiet wisdom of the moment, it felt like more. A symbol.

"You want it?" the clerk asked, her voice soft, yet knowing.

Seven stared at the ticket in her hands. It wasn't just a lottery ticket. It felt like it was meant for her. Without thinking too much, she nodded. "Yeah. I'll take it."

The clerk's smile widened, her eyes gleaming with something unspoken. "Some things are just meant to be, even if we don't understand them at first. Take a chance. Sometimes, the smallest things are the biggest moments."

Seven didn't fully grasp the meaning behind it, but she accepted the ticket, feeling a small thrill ripple through her. The clerk's words held weight, and the strange connection she felt in this moment was more than she could have anticipated.

Later, back in the car, Seven sat with the ticket in her hands. The world outside was beginning to come alive—birds flitting through the trees, their songs a joyful chorus to the changing day. She scratched the ticket, her thoughts swirling, as if she were crossing some threshold into a new phase of her journey.

The numbers appeared slowly, and as she scratched away the final digits, she saw them. 333.

"Three hundred thirty-three..." she whispered to herself, her breath catching.

It wasn't the jackpot. But it felt like something far more profound. A cosmic wink from the universe. A small gift. A sign. Three, threes. It felt significant, like the number itself had power.

The magic was in the simplicity. The three hundred thirty-three wasn't just money. It was a reassurance. It was the universe telling her; you are exactly where you need to be.

Seven let out a deep breath, feeling lighter than she had in days. For the first time in a long time, her shoulders relaxed. The pressure inside her chest dissipated. She didn't need to outrun life anymore. She had found a moment of grace, and it was enough.

She looked up, her eyes scanning the world around her. The birds chirped louder now, and a butterfly fluttered by, its wings delicate, glowing in the soft sunlight. She watched it for a moment, marveling at its beauty.

As if on cue, a ladybug landed on her rearview mirror, and Seven smiled as it gently took flight, rising into the air like a quiet reminder that all things, even the smallest, have a place in this world.

Seven's heart felt full, her chest expanding with a sense of peace. As she rounded a bend in the road, her eyes lifted to the sky.

An eagle soared high above, its wings spread wide, cutting through the air with effortless grace. Seven's heart skipped a beat, her eyes fixed on the bird as it glided through the heavens. There was something powerful about the eagle's flight, its boldness. It was the embodiment of freedom, of soaring above the noise, above the weight of the world.

She watched it until it disappeared into the distance, and as it did, Seven felt a shift inside her. She wasn't running anymore; and she wasn't fleeing the pain. She had stopped. And now she could move forward.

She smiled to herself. The path ahead wasn't perfect, but it was hers to walk. The universe had shown her the way; sometimes, all you needed was to stop and listen.

With a renewed sense of clarity, Seven drove forward. The road stretched out before her, no longer something to fear, but a place to embrace. She was no longer lost. She was exactly where she needed to be.

19

The Still Point

Seven's heart raced as she neared her hometown. Once a place that felt stifling, it now seemed like a different world. Familiar streets and unchanged landmarks passed by, but everything within her had shifted. The weight she'd carried for so long had lifted, leaving space for something lighter: clarity.

The trees lining the streets stood tall and proud, their branches swaying gently in the afternoon breeze, as if welcoming her home. The houses she passed were familiar, each one a snapshot of a past she had run from but now embraced. It was strange, seeing everything so unchanged when she herself had been transformed.

Her mind wandered to Ryan. Her daughter. Her heart. Seven hadn't realized how much she had missed her until now, the thought of seeing her again making her chest tighten with anticipation. Would Ryan be angry? Hurt? Or would she understand that her mother had needed to leave to become better for her?

The road curved gently and her childhood home emerged through the trees. Passed on by her mother, the house had slowly become a part of her future, shaped by her own hands into something that felt entirely hers. The flower beds her mother, Trisha, once fussed over, were replaced by flowers that Ryan chose. The porch was now repainted, and the steps repaired, but the spirit of the place remained. As she pulled closer, a memory ignited, bare feet on the hardwood floors, her mother humming softly, music spilling into every corner of the home, and sunlight spilling through the windows. Now, layered over those moments, was the life she was building, laughter echoing again not just in memory but in presence. It was no longer just a house. It was hers to reclaim, to nurture, to fill with new beginnings.

She parked the car and sat for a moment, gripping the steering wheel as she steadied her breath. This was it. The moment she had dreamed about during her long, lonely nights in the wilderness. The moment she would finally come back, not just to her family, but to herself.

Before she could knock, the door swung open. Trisha stood there, her face a mixture of disbelief, relief, and joy. Her arms opened wide, and before Seven could say a word, she was pulled into a tight embrace.

"You're home," Trisha whispered, her voice breaking with emotion. "We've been so worried about you. We didn't know if you were safe. We even called the police. Your brothers have been asking about you every day. I was so worried."

Seven closed her eyes, letting the warmth of her mother's arms surround her. "I'm sorry, Mom. I didn't mean to scare you. I just... I needed to figure some things out. I needed to breathe."

Trisha pulled back slightly, her hands resting on Seven's shoulders as she studied her daughter's face. "You could've just said that," she said softly, her voice tinged with equal parts relief and exasperation. "We would've given you the space you needed. But disappearing like that? You had all of us worried sick."

"I know," Seven said, her voice steady but full of guilt. "I wasn't trying to hurt anyone. I just didn't know how to say what I needed. But I'm here now. I'm safe. And I'm... better."

Trisha nodded, her eyes glistening with unshed tears. "That's all I need to hear. You're back, and you're okay."

Before Seven could respond, a small voice rang out from the hallway. "Mommy!"

Seven turned sharply, her heart leaping into her throat. Ryan stood there, her little face lighting up with joy as she ran toward her mother. Seven crouched down, her arms wide open, and Ryan barreled into her, wrapping her tiny arms around Seven's neck.

"You're back!" Ryan exclaimed, her voice muffled as she buried her face in Seven's shoulder. "I missed you so much, Mommy!"

Seven held her daughter tightly, tears streaming down her face as she kissed the top of Ryan's head. "I missed you too, baby. More than anything. I'm so sorry I left. I'll never do that again. I promise."

Ryan pulled back slightly, her big, curious eyes locking with Seven's. "Where did you go, Mommy? Did you have an adventure?"

Seven smiled, brushing a strand of hair from Ryan's face. "Something like that. But no adventure is better than being here with you."

Ryan giggled, the sound filling the house with warmth. "Good. Don't go away again, okay?"

"I won't," Seven whispered. "I'll always be here with you and for you."

Trisha watched the scene, her eyes soft with understanding. "You have no idea how much she's missed you, Seven. She cried herself to sleep some nights. But now that you're here, I can see she's already whole again."

"I missed her too, Mom," Seven said, her voice thick with emotion. "She's my everything. She's the reason I found my way back."

Trisha smiled, and in that moment, Seven saw the strength and love her mother had carried all these years. It hadn't always been perfect, but it had always been real.

Family Reunion

The sound of a phone ringing broke the moment, and Trisha quickly answered. "Kase," she said, her voice bubbling with excitement. "Your sister's home. She's safe."

Seven heard Kase's voice on the other end, filled with disbelief. "What? Seven's there? Put her on the phone!"

Trisha hit the speaker button, and Kase's voice boomed through the room. "Seven! What the hell? You've got everyone worried sick, disappearing like that. Mom's been calling everyone and their dog trying to find you."

Seven laughed, the sound light and free. "I'm sorry, Kase. I really am. But I'm back now. I just... I needed some time to figure things out."

"How you gonna just bail on us like that? Don't go leaving me to run this whole circus alone. Next time, at least leave a damn note. Mom's been a wreck, and she was about ready to lose it."

Seven grinned. "Oh, absolutely. The whole circus depends on you, right? Without your legendary leadership, who knows what chaos would break out?"

Kase irritated. "Just don't disappear again, okay? I don't care if you're out there finding yourself or finding Nemo."

Karter's voice came through the speaker, smooth and familiar. "Well, look who finally stopped ghosting the family."

Seven laughed, the sound genuine. "I missed you, Karter."

"Missed you too," he said. "Even if you went full Houdini on us."

"I didn't plan on coming back," she admitted. "But... I'm glad I did."

"I figured," he said. "Was I worried? Yeah. But I trusted you more than the silence scared me."

Her smile softened. "That means everything."

"Yeah, yeah. Save it," he teased. "You still owe me lunch at my favorite spot for emotional damages, of course."

Seven snorted. "Emotional damages, huh?"

"Plus interest," Karter said, grinning in his voice. "But for real... it's good to have you back, Sev."

As the evening settled into a comfortable rhythm, Seven found herself sitting on the back porch with Ryan curled up in her lap. The stars above were brighter than she remembered, each one a reminder of the vastness of the world and her place within it.

Ryan looked up at her, her little face glowing in the moonlight. "Mommy, are you happy now?"

Seven paused, her heart swelling. "I think I am, baby. For the first time in a long time, I feel like I can breathe again."

Ryan smiled, her tiny fingers brushing against Seven's cheek. "Good. I don't want you to feel sad anymore."

Seven kissed her daughter's forehead, her voice soft. "I won't. And even if I do, I'll never leave you. You're my everything, Ryan; always."

As Ryan drifted off to sleep, Seven looked out at the stars, her mind quiet but full. She thought about all the lessons she had learned—about Michael, Rowan, her family, and herself.

These people don't define me, she thought. They're pieces of my story, but I get to decide how it's written.

The road ahead wasn't clear, but that didn't scare her anymore. She wasn't running, nor was she trying to escape. She was ready to take on life one day at a time, and ready to overcome any challenges she may face again.

And as the night deepened, Seven smiled to herself, knowing that this was just the beginning of a new chapter; one where she would finally live, fully and unapologetically.

20

After the Weight

The dining room was alive with the sounds of laughter and warmth. The aroma of freshly baked bread, roasted vegetables, and Trisha's famous sweet potato pie filled the air. Seven sat at the head of the table, her heart swelling as she looked around at the faces of her family. Her brothers, Kase and Karter, traded playful jabs as they passed the dishes, and Ryan's giggles echoed as she tried to balance a roll on her nose, earning a mock scolding from Trisha.

For the first time in a long time, Seven felt whole. The weight of the wilderness, the doubts, and the pain she had carried no longer sat heavy on her shoulders. Instead, she was lighter, freer. The room buzzed with energy, a stark contrast to the quiet solitude she had sought in the woods. This was life in its fullness, messy, loud, imperfect, and beautiful.

As everyone settled, Trisha stood and held up her glass of sweet tea. "Before we dig in, I want to say something," she began, her voice steady but filled with emotion. The chatter faded as the family turned their attention to her.

"God has brought us through a lot this year," Trisha said, her eyes glistening as they landed on Seven. "And tonight, we celebrate more than just being together. We celebrate coming back to what matters: family, love, and resilience. Seven, you scared us half to death, but having you here now..." She paused, her voice catching. "Having you here now is a blessing I'll never take for granted."

The room was silent for a moment, the weight of Trisha's words settling in. Then, one by one, they raised their glasses.

"To family," Kase said, his voice full of warmth. "Even when they drive you crazy."

"To finding yourself," Karter added with a playful grin. "And to having a sister who always has your back, even when she disappears into the woods."

Seven laughed softly, shaking her head. "You're never going to let me live that down, are you?"

"Not a chance," Karter replied, his grin widening.

The room erupted into laughter, and Seven felt the love ripple through her like a wave. She raised her own glass, her hand steady as she spoke. "To life," she said, her voice firm but filled with gratitude. "To learning, growing, and embracing everything it throws at us—the good, the bad, and the messy in-between. We all carry our own weight, but it doesn't have to break us. It can shape us and strengthen us."

Her words hung in the air, and for a moment, the room was still. Then Trisha nodded, her face glowing with pride. "A toast to living," she said softly, and they clinked their glasses together, the sound resonating like a bell tolling a new beginning.

Reflection and Gratitude

Later that evening, after the dishes were cleared and Ryan was tucked into bed, Seven found herself alone on the back porch. The night was quiet; the stars scattered across the sky like diamonds on velvet. A gentle breeze rustled the trees, and the familiar scent of sage from Trisha's garden filled the air.

Seven held her journal in her lap, the pages half-filled with affirmations, reflections, and dreams. She flipped to a blank page and began to write, her pen moving fluidly across the paper.

"Life isn't meant to be perfect. It's meant to be lived. There will be pain, but there will also be joy. There will be mistakes, but there will also be growth. And through it all, we have to remind ourselves that we are enough, just as we are."

She paused, letting the words sink in. Her mind wandered to the journey that had brought her here, the wilderness, the moments of fear, the strangers who had crossed her path and taught her lessons she hadn't been ready to learn.

She thought of the man she had met in the woods, his words still echoing in her mind: "You're not running from the world, you're running from yourself." He had been right. And now, she wasn't running anymore.

Her thoughts turned to her family, the laughter and love that had filled the house tonight. She realized how much she had taken for granted before. The simple joy of Ryan's giggles, the comfort of Trisha's unwavering presence, the teasing camaraderie of her brothers; these were the things that made life rich.

"There are people in the world who would trade places with my problems," Seven whispered to herself. "Wounds take time to heal, but life is a journey. And it's supposed to be messy. It's supposed to be an experience."

She felt a tear slip down her cheek, but it wasn't from sadness. It was from the overwhelming gratitude that filled her heart. She was alive. She was loved; and she was here.

Self-Love and Forgiveness

In the weeks following her return, Seven had journaled every day. It became her sanctuary, a place to explore her thoughts and dreams without judgment. She wrote about the love she wanted to cultivate within herself, the lessons she had learned, and the future she wanted to build.

"I am worthy. I am enough. I am deserving of love," she wrote one evening, the words feeling like a declaration. Each stroke of the pen was a promise to herself, a vow that she would no longer accept anything less than what she deserved.

Forgiveness had also become a cornerstone of her healing. She had written letters to Michael and Rowan, pouring out her pain, her anger, and ultimately, her forgiveness. She didn't send them; she didn't need to. The act of writing was enough.

"I release you," she had written in both letters. "And I release myself."

With every word, she felt the chains of resentment fall away. Forgiving them didn't mean condoning their actions; it meant freeing herself from the burden of carrying that pain. She realized that holding onto anger only kept her tethered to the past, and she was ready to move forward.

A New Dawn

As dawn broke the next morning, Seven stood barefoot in the backyard, the cool grass beneath her feet grounding her. The sky was streaked with hues of orange and pink; the sun rising with quiet majesty.

"I deserve to be happy," she whispered to herself, the words a mantra that had carried her through the darkest moments of her journey.

She thought of Ryan, still asleep inside, and felt a renewed sense of purpose. Her daughter was her anchor, her reason to keep striving, to keep growing. Seven smiled as she imagined the life they would create together, a life filled with laughter, love, and resilience.

The challenges weren't over; she knew that. Life would always have its trials and tribulations. But she had learned to embrace the ebb and flow, to see the beauty in the struggle.

Seven closed her eyes and took a deep breath, the cool morning air filling her lungs. "This is just the beginning," she said softly, the words carrying with them a quiet strength.

As she turned to go back inside, she felt the warmth of hope radiating through her. The past would always be a part of her, but it no longer defined her. She was ready; for love, for growth, for life.

A Toast

That evening, as the family gathered for dinner, Seven raised her glass, her eyes shining with gratitude. "To life," she said, her voice steady and full of emotion. "To living fully, loving deeply, and never letting the weight of the world keep us from seeing its beauty. To resilience, to family, and to the journey."

The glasses clinked, the sound resonating like a bell tolling a new beginning. And in that moment, surrounded by the people she loved most, Seven knew she was exactly where she was meant to be. One day, she might journey again, not to escape, but to grow. And when she did, she'd carry every scar with pride, every lesson like armor, and walk forward with purpose, no longer searching, only becoming.

21

In the Wake of Escape

It's quiet this morning. Peacefully quiet. The kind of quiet that feels like a gentle hug instead of a warning. I'm sitting here with my coffee, still in the clothes I wore to bed, staring out at the dew on the windowpane. The sun hasn't made its way over the trees yet, but there's this stillness I'm grateful for. I'm back. I'm home. And that means something, even if I'm still sorting out what exactly.

I used to think escape was freedom. That slipping out the back door of heartbreak, responsibility, pain, and pressure was liberation. But what I've come to understand is that escape doesn't set you free. It only presses pause. And when you return, everything you tried to outrun is still there, waiting, more patient than you'd ever expect.

Being around family again...it's not perfect. Hell, it's not even close. But last night? That felt good. For a moment, I wasn't the outsider. I wasn't the disappointment or the girl who had to leave to breathe. I was just Seven. Surrounded by people who've known me since my awkward teenage years, who've seen me hurt, heal, stumble, and still keep walking.

There was laughter. Real, unforced laughter. And I don't take that lightly anymore.

It doesn't mean everything's been erased. I know better than to believe that. Coming home doesn't dissolve the tension in the air or the old wounds we try to sweep under the rug. It's more like... learning how to sit with it. I'm trying to be present. Just here. Right now. With my people. Even if some of those dynamics will always be strained.

Take Kase, for instance. I love my brother. Always have. We've just... struggled to meet each other in the middle. Maybe it's that whole sibling rivalry that never got a chance to evolve. Maybe it's deeper. Either way, it still feels like we're fighting childhood ghosts that should've been put to rest years ago. I don't know what it is about us, maybe we're just wired too differently. But I hope, one day, that can change. That we can grow into the kind of siblings who lean on each other instead of sizing each other up.

Then there's Karter. Solid. That's the only way I know how to describe him. He's one of the few constants in my life. Which is wild, considering he's my little brother. He gets me in a way most people don't. Even when we disagree, and we do, our communication has this maturity to it that I'm proud of. I lean on him more than he probably knows. And when I think about the people I can truly count on, Karter is always on that list. Always.

And my dad. Or rather, my biological dad, Derek. We don't talk much. That's not new. I think a part of him is still trying to forgive himself for not being the father he should've been. Maybe it's guilt. Maybe it's pride. Maybe both. I can't pretend to know. But I feel it, the distance. And I think he does too. Some days I want to call him out, scream at him, ask why he didn't try harder. Other days, I feel for him. I think he avoids me, not because he doesn't care, but because he does—and it hurts him to face that part of his past.

I don't hate him. I never have and we are oddly very similar, other than the fact that I look just like him. He wasn't the worst dad. He contributed where he could, just not in the ways I needed most. He was a half-ass dad. And I say that with all the love and pain tangled up in those words. It's crazy, really. How sometimes your stepdad can become more of a father figure than the man who gave you life. Life's full of contradictions like that.

And let's be honest. I'm not perfect either. I've said shit I shouldn't have. I've hurt people, sometimes without realizing it. Sometimes fully aware and too stubborn to stop myself. But I've grown. And I'm still growing. At my core, my intentions have always been good. I care deeply. Sometimes too deeply. And that makes things messy. But I'm working on myself, piece by piece.

I look at some of the friendships I have now, and I wonder: are these lifelong friendships? Or are they placeholders? Some of them feel like they're stuck in 2015, like we never evolved. Like I outgrew a version of myself that they still expect to see. And that's hard. Because I love them. But love doesn't always mean longevity. I don't know if I'm supposed to walk away completely, or if these relationships just need time and grace to transform.

And then there's Trisha, my mom. Whew!

That woman... I don't even know where to start. We've never had the kind of mother-daughter bond I used to see on TV. You know, the ones where they're best friends, giggling over wine, sharing secrets. That's not us. Ours has always been more... strained. Complex. She did the best she could as a single mom, and I don't take that for granted. I really don't. But I can't pretend that there aren't scars from the way we clash. From the way she'd dismiss my feelings or try to shape me into who she thought I should be.

Still, I love her. And even though I don't have much hope that our relationship will ever be what I wish it could, I've accepted that. I've made peace with the version of our bond that exists. And if it never gets deeper than this, then that's just something I'll have to carry with me.

But last night gave me a gleam of something different. Something warmer. It reminded me that home, even when it's chaotic, can still be healing.

I keep thinking about Ryan. About what she sees when she looks at me. I want to be better for her. I want her to have memories that aren't stained by secrets or disappointments. I want her to see what real love looks like—not the performative, Instagram-worthy kind, but the kind that stays when it's inconvenient. The kind that holds space for imperfection. The kind that shows up.

And Rowan? He'll never be that. He was my own version of my father, a man who showed up halfway and called it love.

When I confronted him, it wasn't the explosive moment you'd expect. No shouting. No slamming doors. Just silence. That silence spoke louder than any lie he ever told. I remember the way he avoided eye contact, how his voice got small when I asked him how long he'd been married. He didn't even try to fight it. He just stood there like a coward. I remember thinking, this man doesn't even have the decency to lie with conviction anymore.

I walked out of that room changed. Not broken, changed. My love for him didn't die all at once. It withered. Quietly. Every time he didn't show up. Every time he let me carry the weight alone. Every time he pretended he was something he wasn't.

He was a placeholder in my life. A body that temporarily filled a void. But my daughter? She's not temporary. She's not something you just forget.

And now I'll never understand how he could disappear so completely. I've stopped trying to. I have no answers. Only responsibility. And I'll carry that with pride.

Sometimes, in the middle of the night, I wake up with this heavy feeling in my chest. Like something's coming. Like danger is waiting on the other side of a door I haven't opened yet. I hear noises sometimes, strange creaks, a car that idles outside a little too long. Maybe it's paranoia. Maybe it's my body warning me that the past has a way of circling back. I don't know. But I'm not stupid. I know there are things out there that can unravel you if you're not careful.

Last week I had a dream I was drowning. Not in water, but in shadows. The harder I tried to climb out, the more the darkness pulled me under. And then, just before I gave in, I felt a hand. Ryan's hand. Tiny. Firm. Pulling me back to the surface.

That's what she is. My anchor. My second chance.

I know now that healing doesn't mean forgetting. It means facing the mess, holding it close, and still choosing to move forward.

And yeah, I've thought about leaving. Starting over somewhere new. But not to run away, not anymore. If I ever decide to go, it'll be because I'm ready. Because I'm healed. Because it's the right move, not a desperate escape. I owe myself that much. I owe Ryan that much.

I'm allowed to move on. I'm allowed to build something different. But I want to do it the right way with clarity, with purpose, with peace in my heart.

So this morning, as I sit here in the soft light of a brand new day, I feel... okay. Not perfect. Not whole. But okay.

And that's more than enough. And with that, I am happy. I am content.

Because despite the chaos, the heartbreak, the fractures in my relationships, there is still love. There is still hope. There is still me.

Seven.